'Look at me!'

Jorja slowly raised her face, knowing it to be naked with uncertainty.

'You've gone quite pale,' Renzo mused. 'I shall ask you again what I asked you before, do you find the thought of my lovemaking so repellent?'

'I—don't know.'

'You must know.' His voice had hardened. 'You must feel something when I touch you.'

'Yes.' The word broke from her. 'I can't stop thinking that it's Angelica you want to—hold in your arms. I don't like to think of being used as a substitute for her!'

'Ah, we are back to that again. Forget your sister once and for all. Let us both forget her very existence—so!'

The warm exhalation of his breath was against Jorja's face, and then he was kissing her slowly, his lips stroking sensuously over hers. 'Don't do this to me,' she wanted to plead. 'Don't make me like what you're doing to me . . .'

THE HONEYMOON

BY

VIOLET WINSPEAR

MILLS & BOON LIMITED
15–16 BROOK'S MEWS
LONDON W1A 1DR

First published in Hardback in Great Britain in 1986
by Worldwide Romance

This Paperback edition published in 1986
by Mills & Boon Limited,
15–16 Brook's Mews, London W1A 1DR

Australian copyright 1986
Philippine copyright 1986

© Violet Winspear 1986

ISBN 0 263 75472 3

09/0786–60,100

Set in 11 on 12 pt Linotron Palatino

Photoset by Rowland Phototypesetting Limited
Bury St Edmunds, Suffolk
Printed and bound in Great Britain by
Cox & Wyman, Reading

. . . my heart shall grow
Too close against thy heart to henceforth know
Its separate trembling pulse . . .

Elizabeth Barrett Browning

CHAPTER ONE

'CUT the cake!' everyone chorused.

And with his ambiguous smile the bridegroom plunged a knife into the white icing of the wedding cake, evoking cheers and laughter from the throng of guests assembled in this hotel reception room overlooking the Marble Arch.

One person in the room could have hurled the iced cake to the floor and trampled into pieces the silver horseshoe and the bells . . . that person was the bride of Renzo Talmonte.

In her classic gown of satin and lace she looked the traditional bride but inside Jorja was seething with emotion. The Reverend Michael Norman had chosen not to attend the wedding and she felt such a sense of injustice. She was here, with an unfamiliar ring on her left hand, in order to save her father from knowing that his beloved Angelica wasn't the angel he believed her to be.

When Renzo Talmonte had come to Jorja in the garden of the rectory and shown her the letters which her sister had written to his brother, she could have choked with shame. Their erotica had been mingled with wild pleadings that Stelvio leave his wife and child. Outpourings of passion and possession which drove Jorja to rip the pages into shreds.

'Those were copies,' Renzo informed her, and there among the roses of her father's garden Jorja saw the ruthless intention in his Latin eyes. 'She has run off with Stelvio, and I intend to be married by the time the affair has burned itself out. I shall be her sister's husband—your husband.'

His words made no sense at first, then as Jorja felt their impact she backed away in panic from the lean Italian in the well-cut suit. 'You're crazy!' she exclaimed, and found herself flinching when he slightly raised the ebony stick which he carried. It seemed to add menace to his personality that a long-ago accident had left him with a leg which was noticeably less supple than the rest of him.

When Angelica had brought him to the rectory to meet her family, he had surprised Jorja deeply. She had always known that her sister wanted to marry a good-looking man, but Renzo Talmonte displayed the breeding of a very old name, and it seemed to Jorja that he had a lot more in his head than her sister would ever appreciate.

Upon being introduced to Jorja he had raised her hand and brushed it lightly with his lips. Their eyes had met and because she was unaccustomed to men of his stamp she could well have betrayed her thoughts. Thoughts she shouldn't have entertained . . . that he was far too deep, and possibly too attached to a Latin code of morality to be the right man for Angelica.

Had he read her eyes that day . . . or misread

them? Did he imagine that she, the stay-at-home daughter, had developed a hopeless crush on him? Was that why they now stood among the litter of her sister's love letters and he told her so purposely that he meant to marry her?

Even if she had thought him mentally superior to Angelica, the contrast in their colouring had struck her as rather beautiful. For days the image of them together had haunted her.

'Think over what I've proposed.' He studied Jorja there among the roses, taking in her sunlit hair, framing casually the reserved charms of her features. His eyes rested on the softly shaded hollow of her throat, where her quickened breathing stirred a slim gold cross on a chain. Her fingers sought the cross, as if for reassurance.

'In a week's time,' he said, 'you can tell me if I'm to show Angelica's letters to your father. Their salacious detail should come as quite a shock to him.'

It was a week of unbearable tension for Jorja; she prayed that he would come to his senses and stay away. But on the Saturday morning he arrived as promised and once again they confronted each other, the scent of the roses heavy on the air after a fall of rain.

Jorja had no answer for him as he stood waiting for one. 'Don't mistake me,' he stirred fallen rose petals with the ferrule of his stick, 'the original letters are in my car and I'm sure your father will recognise their handwriting. He has a strict code of morals, has he not? Such a pity he failed to impose them upon your sister, though I don't think they've been lost on you. You have your share of the virtues.'

'Your own virtue seems sadly lacking, *signore*, when you come here making threats that could break my father's heart.'

'You can so easily keep it intact, *signorina*. You marry me!'

'You're blackmailing me——' In reaching out as if to support a feeling of insecurity Jorja closed her hand on a rose bough laden with thorns. They hurt cruelly as they pierced her flesh, and she had to allow Renzo to remove the thorns with meticulous care, his dark head bent to her fair one. After binding her hand in his speckless handkerchief he took her into the house, and without giving her a chance he told her father they were going to be married.

'But I don't understand——' The Reverend Michael Norman gazed at Renzo in astonishment. 'First you want Angelica for your wife and now the engagement is broken you want to take Jorja away from me.'

'You can't keep Jorja always tied to housekeeping in this old house, with no life of her own to enjoy.' As Renzo spoke, Jorja wanted to protest against his every word. She tried to speak but the clamour inside her wouldn't make itself audible.

'You permitted Angelica to go out into the world,' Renzo said, in the faultless English of the well-bred foreigner.

'That was different,' Jorja's father argued.

'How was it different.' Renzo laid a firm hand on Jorja's shoulder and compelled her to remain in the chair where he had seated her. His touch seemed to run down her arm and join the throbbing of her hand within the cool folds of his handkerchief.

'Angelica didn't wish to remain at home.' The Reverend Michael cast a frown at Jorja. 'Though my daughters look alike, they have always had different ways. Please inform this man, Jorja, that your duty to me comes before marriage to him —the entire idea is untenable. I can't possibly give my permission!'

'Jorja has given hers.' The lean hand pressed relentlessly upon her shoulder, warning of what he would do if she dared to defy him. With that chin, and those eyes, he looked proud as the Devil and Jorja didn't doubt that his pride had been injured by Angelica's behaviour . . . perhaps even his heart, for she presumed he had one.

She sat there, feeling torn between the will of the two men, biting back the words she was afraid to make audible.

'You must know of a woman who will come to the rectory to keep house for you,' Renzo spoke to her father. 'Jorja has come to the time when she must live her own life.'

'Will you please say something.' The Reverend Michael had his eyes fixed upon Jorja, as if compelling her to the obedience she had always shown him. 'You aren't going to leave me—you can't!'

'Come, *cara mia*,' Renzo's fingers renewed their warning against the fine bones of her shoulder, 'tell your father that you are going to become my wife.'

She glanced up at him and saw the threat smouldering at the centres of his Latin eyes. Oh God, she didn't know how to cope with a man so ruthless and determined; her life had been restricted to a rectory in a country village where the daily pattern of life didn't get disturbed in this way. All she could be certain of was that he would disillusion her father about Angelica if she refused to comply with his outrageous demand on her.

If she refused him, her sister would be exposed and her father would be bitterly hurt. To all outward appearance Angelica was the living image of their mother, and Daddy had loved her so dearly. Ever since her death he had seen her face and form reflected in Angelica.

'Yes—I have agreed.' Jorja heard the words as if they came from someone else, for her voice sounded so strained as she spoke them. They were like words spoken in a dream, they were so unreal.

For long moments her father gazed at her in silence, then at last he spoke, almost as if he were intoning a sermon from the pulpit. 'I would never have believed that a child of mine could betray me as you are doing.'

'You will not use that word.' Renzo suddenly became angry, so that every feature of his Latin face was even more detailed. His look made

Jorja realise that he did have feelings and they were still raw from Angelica's betrayal of him.

Dismay clutched physically at Jorja. He had lost Angelica not only to his brother, but to Italian principles which were probably more deep in his bones than in Stelvio's. Though Angelica was the substance of his desire, Jorja was there in the flesh, her very attachment to her family making it possible for Renzo to bring about a marriage based on emotional blackmail.

Jorja glanced from him to her father. The moment was hers, she could spell it all out and she wouldn't have to stand at the altar with a stranger and make vows about honouring and cherishing someone she neither knew nor loved.

Her lips worked and she heard her own strained voice again. 'Aunt Beatrice will come and take care of you, Daddy. You know how much she dislikes that hotel where she's living.'

'You are my daughter,' he said sternly. 'I have relied on you.'

'Daughters are made for more than lifelong duty to a parent,' Renzo said curtly. 'The attitude is a selfish one, that a daughter should be denied a husband and children.'

Evocative words which made Jorja realise what it would mean to be married to Renzo Talmonte. In no way was he suggesting a platonic relationship. He meant the marriage to be fully realised . . . he meant her to be a wife in all that the word implied.

Her fingers clenched over the hand which had

been stabbed by thorns in the garden, and she almost welcomed the pain, for it seemed to numb her fears.

'What have you done to your hand?' her father abruptly asked.

'I—I tore it on a rose bush, Daddy.'

His face registered no sympathy. 'Be warned,' he said, 'thorns will tear more than your hand if you marry this man who has courted your sister.'

Jorja caught her breath. 'Oh, Daddy——' She desperately wanted him to know that she was protecting his feelings. That she was saving him from ever finding out that Angelica was far from being the angel he liked to call her.

How unfair it was that love for her father tied her tongue, while Renzo's need for reparation made him so bitterly arrogant, so determined to show Angelica that she could be quickly and easily replaced by her younger sister.

And six weeks later he had his way, and in the limousine which drove them to the wedding reception he drew Jorja into his arms and showed her with his kiss that even if she responded with no more warmth than a figure of ice, he would melt her when the time came.

'A pity your father chose not to attend our wedding,' he said. 'I feel certain you wanted him there to give you away.'

'Did you really suppose that he would attend?' She drew as far away as his strong arm would permit and with cool blue eyes she regarded him in his perfect grey suit. Oh, there was no denying his looks. If today he had married Angelica and she had been a guest at their wedding, then she would have thought him a handsome and distinguished bridegroom.

To everyone in the church he must have seemed so, and no one who pelted them with confetti had any idea that those delicate rose petals and horseshoes had felt like pellets of ice beating against her satin and lace.

There at the reception she stood among the wedding guests and felt as if she were alone on an island. The laughter and the speeches came to her from a distance, and if she was deemed a little quiet, then those who knew Angelica supposed that she was thinking of how quickly she had stepped into her sister's wedding shoes.

'You look in need of champagne.' A flute of the golden wine was placed in her hand. 'I feel I can tell you to drink down every drop as I gave you away to Renzo.'

She met Bruce Clayton's eyes and managed a brief smile. He and Renzo were both in the business of making films. Bruce directed many of the big productions for which Renzo composed his stunning music. A labour of love for Renzo whose main source of income derived from his investments in film and recording companies. On the surface he seemed detached from the world of commerce, but it was only a façade. His shrewd investments in successful companies had made him a very wealthy man.

He had made it his business to tell Jorja certain things about himself. He came from an ancient

Roman family which in days gone by had lived in palaces on the banks of the Tiber. But the Talmonte fortunes had fluctuated down the years until very little was left in the coffers for Renzo and his brother. Only a trust fund which enabled them to be educated, a few pieces of family jewellery and the remains of a wine cellar.

The two young men had made their own fortunes. Renzo, with a natural ability to create music, had gravitated towards the composition of it and investment in the industry itself. Stelvio had become a successful lawyer, and it seemed to add to Renzo's bitterness that his brother should risk his career and his marriage, and prove himself less than trustworthy, by indulging in a love affair which had created unhappiness for all concerned.

Jorja sipped her champagne, which on an empty stomach was making her head go round. Something in the way she looked at him made Bruce Clayton go to the buffet where he took a plate and forked ham and chicken salad on to it. He returned to Jorja's side with the food and insisted that she eat it.

'I don't think I could——' She broke off and gave a slight hiccup. 'Oops, I think I'm getting tiddly. The rector's daughter isn't used to ch-champagne.'

'Come and sit down and eat some lunch.' Bruce propelled her into an alcove where a chair stood vacant. 'You'd better not be tiddly when Renzo finally detaches himself from Connie Caswell. I guess she's pumping him for something she can use in her gossip column.'

'It would make for gossip, wouldn't it, Bruce?' Jorja pushed the food around the plate. 'Within two months of his broken engagement to a lovely model, well-known Italian composer weds her sister! It's bound to make the t-tongues wag. I bet everyone in this room is thinking that I've worked fast.'

'A few of us are thinking that Renzo's struck lucky,' Bruce Clayton said quietly. His eyes dwelt on her face, framed by the bridal headdress which brought into focus a certain look which made other women in the room seem jaded and over-painted.

'The majority are thinking that I've struck lucky,' Jorja murmured, and her gaze dwelt upon Renzo, his free arm in the grip of Connie Caswell's hand, tipped with bloodred fingernails. Renzo leaned on his stick as he listened to the woman's endless chatter, and something in his stance made Jorja wonder if his leg was aching. In brusque tones he had told her about his leg. It had been smashed in a riding accident; the horse had rolled on him and the surgeon had wanted to amputate because the fractures were so bad. He was eighteen at the time and his mother insisted that the broken bones be re-set and the leg put in plaster.

The results had been less than satisfactory and ever since Renzo had assisted the leg with a walking stick. He had freely admitted to Jorja that as a youth he had hated his disability but the passage of the years had made him more tolerant of it. At least, he said, he didn't have to prove his machismo by competing with the squash players and the joggers. The leg didn't stop him from swimming or playing bridge.

'Do try and eat a few bites of food,' Bruce Clayton urged. 'How about a slice of your own cake—it looks delicious.'

She shook her head with a shudder. 'It would choke me,' she exclaimed.

'Look, I'm worried about you.' Bruce hunched down until his eyes were on a level with hers. 'I know it's customary for a bride to be jittery on her wedding day but you seem positively—reluctant.'

'Do I?' Her gaze wavered away from his; he had observant green eyes and she was afraid he was seeing more than he should. 'I've lived a quiet life, you know, and there must be at least a hundred people in this room. You and Renzo are used to the high life, but all these smart people with their smart talk are confusing to me.'

'Is that all that's bothering you?' Bruce persisted.

'Why should anything bother me?' And so saying she speared a piece of chicken and green pepper and forced the food between her lips. 'Apart from the fact that I'm a country girl who has just been married to a sophisticated man. Living with Renzo isn't going to be the same as living in a rectory—you see, I only look like Angelica. We're poles apart in temperament.'

'Do you really think you look like her?' Bruce gave Jorja an intent look.

'Renzo thinks I look like her.' With a supreme effort Jorja ate a piece of ham and tomato. 'He couldn't have the original so he's settled for the copy, and as we all know a copy always lacks the true value in the eyes of the owner.'

'Is that how you think of Renzo, as your owner?' Bruce was frowning and his gaze had settled on the gold wedding band that was gemmed with sapphires, quite obviously chosen to reflect the azure of Jorja's eyes.

'Look at him, Bruce, doesn't it show that ownership runs in his veins? He's a Talmonte and they trace their line back to the days of Roman supremacy. His name is in the history books alongside the name of Borgia.'

When Bruce caught his breath Jorja realised that she was giving away a little too much of her feelings, and she forced a laugh. 'I—I suppose I'm a little unhappy because my father refused to attend the wedding. I've always looked after him, you see, and he was hurt that I should leave him. He thought I was content to remain at home——'

Jorja suppressed a sigh. Now and again she had envied Angelica's freedom but for the most part she had been content. Duncton lay in a Sussex vale and the surrounding countryside was lovely; it hadn't occurred to her to even think of marriage until Renzo's eruption into her life. She and everyone in the village had assumed that she would always take care of her father and remain a spinster in the tradition of stay-at-home daughters.

Abruptly Bruce straightened up and Jorja became aware that Renzo was approaching the alcove, walking towards her with the aid of his stick and yet still managing to look upright and commanding. It flashed through her mind to wonder what kind of a man he would have been if the riding accident had not disabled him. Would he have been more carefree and less aloof, as if in learning to control all the pain which his leg had caused him, he had become insensitive to other people's pain.

'Are you ready to go on your honeymoon?' he asked in his sardonic way. 'If so, then you had better go with Flavia to change out of your gown.'

Flavia was his personal assistant, who had arranged the reception and booked their stay at Duke's Hotel in Sandbourne on the Sussex coast. She was hovering just beyond Renzo's shoulder, a tall redhead who still managed to look businesslike in a pearly-grey suit with a pink carnation pinned to the lapel.

'I——' Jorja looked around for somewhere to set down the plate of half-eaten food. Bruce took it from her hand and gave her the slightest of encouraging nods. She stood up and found Renzo quite near to her; their eyes met and her fears leapt to the surface as she stood there and felt his personality and his force sweep over her. This stranger was her husband and quite soon she would be quite alone with him.

'Well,' he spoke with a touch of mockery,

'aren't you eager to get to the seaside? It was your idea, after all.' He glanced at Bruce, who was regarding the two of them with a touch of perplexity. 'When I asked this girl if she would like to visit the Caribbean for the honeymoon she informed me that she very much liked an English resort called Sandbourne. That when she was young and her mother was alive they would go there for the summer vacation. Very well, I said, if you prefer the uncertain English weather to the balmy breezes of the tropics then we shall go to this childhood paradise.'

He returned his eyes to Jorja's pensive face. 'Paradise awaits us, and you stand there as if glued to the floor. If you don't go this second to change your gown then I shall take you as you are.'

'I'm going.' She cast a quick, uncertain smile at Bruce, then snatching above her ankles the full satin skirt of her wedding gown she hastened from the room with Flavia, hearing a renewal of claps and cheers as the guests realised that the bride was about to change into her going away outfit.

Flavia opened the door of the bedroom where Jorja was to change. The dress in delphinium blue was laid out on the bed, and the ivory cashmere coat was still on its hanger. The rest of her trousseau was in pigskin baggage in the boot of the handsome veteran Rolls-Royce which Renzo drove. It had a magnificent engine and he maintained that the car almost drove itself. Panelled in rich woods, upholstered in glove-soft hide, it was equipped with a music-centre instead of a cocktail cabinet.

Very carefully Flavia assisted Jorja out of the satin gown. 'How does it feel to be married?' she asked.

Jorja removed the long satin underslip and shivered as she bared her shoulders. How could she say that she felt nothing but a crushing loneliness for the life she had left in order to marry a stranger?

'I feel a little—detached,' she said, 'but that could be the effects of the champagne. I'd never had it until today.'

'Truly?' Flavia smiled slightly but not in an unkind way. 'Anyone can see that you've led a blameless life—let me secure those little hooks for you.'

The material of the blue dress was French jersey of the very best quality; everything that Renzo had insisted on providing for her trousseau was of the very best. It wasn't only that he had a lot of money to spend but she had quickly realised that he was a man of impeccable taste. With a discerning eye he had selected every garment of her honeymoon clothes, and at each fitting Jorja had been amazed by her own appearance in the long mirrors.

It wasn't that he made her wear garments that would have been Angelica's choice, but he chose fabrics and colours that befitted Jorja's own personality. Soft, fine, casual things whose simplicity concealed their cost.

'This colour does become you,' Flavia

remarked, and she retreated a few steps in order to study Jorja. 'You reflect certain aspects of your sister, and yet you're different.'

Jorja stepped into the shoes that matched her dress. Did the people who were less close than Bruce know what Angelica had done to Renzo, or had he managed to conceal the true facts? She suspected that for his brother's sake he had managed to save the affair from becoming a public scandal; there was also his sister-in-law and the child to consider.

'Angelica has always been the outgoing one.' Jorja tried to sound casual as she sat at the dressing-table and ran a comb through the simple styling of her hair. A vase of flowers stood beside her and she breathed the scent of yellow tulips mingling with carnations and irises. She felt the scent creeping into her brain and senses, as if storing itself away.

'It was a good thing they realised their incompatibility before getting married, Renzo being a Catholic.' The wedding dress rustled as Flavia carefully folded it. 'I'll take your gown to Hanson Square while you're away, Jorja, along with the accessories and the veil. And what would you like me to do about letters if any arrive for you at the house? Shall I send them on to the hotel?'

Jorja wondered if her father would relent and write to her. She sorely hoped that he would. It would be unbearable if he chose to treat her as if she had betrayed him.

'If I do receive any mail, then I would like you to send it on to me.' Jorja stood up and felt the soft clinging of the jersey-silk dress, and this added to the sense of unreality she couldn't shake off. Her attire at the rectory had been neat shirts with a skirt or a pair of trousers, and it had been necessary to make her clothes endure. Now, at Renzo's insistence, she had more than she could possibly need . . . a dream come true for many a girl but Jorja felt trapped.

She avoided looking again in the mirror because her hair was the same pale gold as her sister's. She didn't want to look into her own eyes because they were the same deep blue. Even in her slenderness of build she resembled Angelica.

'I'm the copy,' she had told Bruce Clayton. 'Renzo couldn't have the original so he married me.'

The silk lining of her coat struck cool against her arms and when she shivered Flavia looked at her with a touch of concern. 'Becoming a bride is more enjoyable for the guests, isn't it, Jorja?'

'It is,' Jorja spoke fervently, her fingers tensed upon the stylish crocodile handbag into which Renzo had dropped such items as a crocodile wallet, a gold pen, a gold key-fob, and a mother-of-pearl compact and perfume spray. She had found money in the wallet, a car key on the fob, and a Chanel perfume in the spray. Such a man would be generous to equal his cruelty . . . there stalked in his Roman blood distant echoes of the Christians torn to ribbons by lions.

When she wryly smiled, Flavia patted her hand. 'That's better, my dear. Those people out there will be expecting a smile, and as you may have noticed the Caswell woman has eyes like a hawk. She's the terror of Fleet Street in those outlandish hats of hers, and she can blow the merest flicker of gossip into a flame. I know your sister's on your mind, but smile, for Renzo's sake.'

'Yes, it's all for his sake, isn't it?' With that thought in mind Jorja rejoined her bridegroom amid a crowd of people who were just as strange to her as he was.

One face alone in that crowd gave her a slight lift of the heart, for as she met Bruce Clayton's eyes, he lowered the lid of his left eye in a wink of understanding.

He was so opposite to Renzo, whose distinguished good looks were unnerving as he drew her ringed hand into the crook of his arm.

'Ladies and gentlemen,' he said, 'Jorja and I have an urgent appointment so we have to leave you. We thank you for coming to see us married.'

'It was a pleasure, darling.' Connie Caswell laughed. 'You two have given me my best story for weeks.'

'I feel sure we have,' Renzo retorted, and as he spoke Jorja felt the tension in his body. So for him, as well as for her, the wedding had been something of an ordeal. He had managed to conceal his inner feelings well, but it was obvious that he must have been thinking all the time of Angelica.

Jorja tilted her chin in a proud way. Well, he had asked for any unhappiness that he felt . . .

any regret that he had forced her to share a marriage when not a spark of love existed between them.

'Throw the bouquet,' someone called out.

Flavia handed it to her and with almost a gesture of wanting to throw away the marriage that went with the flowers, Jorja tossed the bunch of rosebuds and freesias into the crowd. Someone caught it, she didn't know who, for Renzo was suddenly hurrying her away with him.

'Do have fun, darlings.' The suggestive voice of Connie Caswell followed them. 'Send me a postcard from Sandbourne—if you find the time.'

Renzo muttered something in his own language, and it came as a relief to Jorja to find herself inside the Rolls-Royce, which the doorman had kept under surveillance. It wasn't strewn with ribbons as they drove away in the rain which kept most of the guests inside the foyer of the hotel.

'It was bound to rain.' Renzo gestured in a very Latin way as they waited at some traffic signals. 'We could have flown into the sun, had you been willing.'

She cast a glance at his profile . . . did he imagine that she was ever going to be a willing participant? Her eyes as she looked at him were as gem-hard as the sapphires in her ring. All she saw was a man who had blackmailed her into marriage with him . . . a man who felt driven to punish everyone who was connected with the girl who had gone behind his back with his brother.

Latin people were like that, so she understood. They practised a form of vendetta which extended to the members of the family, and already he had caused a serious rift between her and her father . . . a rift she could hardly bear to think about.

Renzo Talmonte made his home in England, but from the crown of his dark head down to the soles of his well-shod feet he was an Italian, and today in the guise of a bridegroom he had carried his vendetta a step further, and Jorja watched him smile to himself.

What were his thoughts as he drove through the city traffic? It seemed to Jorja that he was finding pleasure in them, as if so far his plan of revenge had gone smoothly and he could anticipate the next torment he had in store for her.

'Everything went off very well,' he remarked. 'Flavia's an excellent organiser and I wouldn't know what to do without her.'

'It's a pity you didn't marry her!' Jorja's emotions were so overwrought that she needed to let off some steam after the ordeal of being married to a man who didn't love her. 'Why did you have to destroy my life—what did I ever do to you?'

'A short while ago you became my wife,' he retorted. 'You stood at the altar looking like a bride figure carved out of white icing. That is how Connie Caswell described you. She even had the audacity to ask me if we love each other.'

'Oh, and what did you say?' Jorja stared through the windscreen and watched the raindrops being swept back and forth by the blades. People hastened along the pavements, umbrellas aslant in the gusty rain, and the traffic was heavy along Piccadilly. Drivers honked and hooted but there was a deliberate calm about Renzo.

'I told the woman that I never discuss my personal feelings.'

'You'd hardly tell her, Renzo, that we barely know each other—that our motivation for marriage is your . . . hatred.'

'I have heard it said, Jorja, that hate and love are as inseparable as night and day. That you can't have one without the other.'

'I don't believe it,' Jorja spoke tensely. 'Night and day are distinct from each other, you can tell them apart. The same goes for love and hate, you can tell one from the other quite easily.'

He manoeuvred the car into the stream of traffic heading towards the Embankment. 'Don't stop there, Jorja. I find your theory of immense fascination.'

She didn't care if he was being sardonic and spoke with feeling. 'W-when you love someone you want to be with him. When you hate someone you want to be anywhere but in his company. I think you can guess how I feel, Renzo.'

'Indubitably. You would like to be anywhere but driving with me to Sandbourne—I thought you liked the place?'

'I like it enormously but I don't expect to enjoy myself on this occasion,' she said distantly.

'Too bad, *cara mia*.' He spoke casually. 'I intend to enjoy myself . . . strange to say, although I've had a house in England for some time, I have never visited one of your seaside resorts. I am looking forward to the experience.'

'With a wife who can't stand the sight of you?' Jorja was using words like pointed pins and she enjoyed digging them into him. It was her only means of defence. Renzo wouldn't find her an easy victim of his vendetta.

'My effect upon you, Jorja, is of little consequence,' he replied. 'It is your effect upon me which matters.'

Jorja absorbed the meaning in his words and felt a hot stinging in her cheeks. The buildup of emotion was almost more than she could bear and for a wild moment she wanted to grab the wheel and wrench the car into the kerb. She wanted to give way to emotion and not care about the consequences, but an image of the ivy-hung rectory at Duncton was so clear in her mind. She visualised her father at work upon a sermon in the oak-lined study, an aroma of steak and kidney pie drifting from the kitchen which had been her domain for such a long time.

She couldn't shatter Daddy's world; it was bad enough that he wouldn't speak to her because he believed she had let him down.

'You'll regret this day, Renzo,' she said, and she huddled away from him in the cashmere coat, despising the fine clothes he had forced upon her.

'I don't want you looking like a domestic,' he had said, when he had taken her to the fashion house where a staircase of marble led to a salon of mirrors, reflecting her figure from every angle. The eyes of the sales ladies had appraised her as if she were a gauche filly he wanted them to train.

'I detest you,' she declared.

'Then how fortunate that I don't love you,' he drawled.

'Things are bad enough without your wretched love!' She watched the rain run down the windows of the car like teardrops. 'You're in love with Angelica but none of this is hurting her. The ones you're hurting are here in this car.'

'Is that so?' He spoke without emotion.

'You know it is!' Jorja said fiercely.

'You didn't have to marry me—I gave you a choice.'

'Some choice!' Jorja gave him a scornful look. 'When you first met me, *signore*, you had me summed up as the kind of daughter most people despise. Protective and caring of my father and not too bothered about having fun all the time, because, as Daddy told you, Angelica and I were never alike in ways. You saw the contrast that first time you came to Duncton, you knew I had no choice from the moment you spoke about your being my husband. You knew I couldn't hurt my father.'

'Of course I knew it.' Renzo spoke dispassionately. 'I would not have come to Duncton had I not known it.'

'My God,' Jorja's eyes dwelt upon him unbelievingly, 'there has to be a name for a man like you.'

'*Homme sans merci*, as the French say.'

'Man without mercy.' Jorja breathed the words and thought how well they applied to him.

'*Si.*'

CHAPTER TWO

THE porter lifted out the pigskin luggage from the boot of the Rolls, and Jorja walked beside her husband into the reception hall of Duke's Hotel, a dominating feature of the wide esplanade with its banks of flowers.

In days gone by, when Jorja used to come to Sandbourne with her family, this majestic hotel had been a kind of palace to be admired from a distance. When the smartly dressed men and women emerged for their outings Angelica would say that one day she would stay at hotels like it and wear the very latest styles.

It was no wonder that Jorja felt bemused as she stood there while Renzo signed the register and made various enquiries. It seemed hardly believable that it was she, the unassuming daughter of the Reverend Michael Norman, who had come to stay at Duke's. Her glance travelled the tall marble columns to an ornate ceiling hung with chandeliers. She noticed the old-fashioned lift in a cage of wrought-iron, and the arcaded lounge where some of the guests sat in cane chairs and enjoyed afternoon tea.

Jorja was longing for a cup of tea, and her wistful glance into the tea lounge must have caught Renzo's attention for he told the porter to take up their luggage and pressed a generous tip into his hand.

'Come along.' Renzo took Jorja by the elbow and led her to a cane table for two. 'I haven't the heart to ignore such an imploring look in your eyes.'

As they sat down, Jorja was aware that they were being studied by people at the adjacent tables and she was glad that neither of them showed any sign of having been married so recently. Renzo ordered a pot of tea and a selection of cakes from the waitress and he looked so at ease in these grand surroundings that he might have been a married man for years.

Jorja relaxed and drew off her gloves in softest kidskin and exactly the colour of her shoes. She let her coat slide off her shoulders on to the cane back of her chair and tried not to notice the comprehensive look which Renzo gave her; a look which took in her hair, her mouth, and the slim, pale column of her neck in contrast to the blue dress.

Was she reminding him of Angelica? They had been engaged for several months so inevitably they had shared meals together, and being two people of the world they might have stayed at hotels as lovers.

It was a thought she didn't wish to dwell on, for it emphasised Angelica's treachery towards him and made her feel more afraid than ever of the emotions that were banked down under his urbane manner. Despite the handicap of his leg he was a physically strong man, the fine grey

cloth of his suit tailored across wide shoulders
. . . she would be no match for him if he released
pent-up, bitter passions upon her when they
were alone in their hotel suite with the door
closed upon the world.

'Aren't you going to be mother and pour the
tea?' he drawled.

'Yes—of course.' She lifted the teapot and by
an effort of will managed to pour tea into the cups
without spilling it all over the table. She knew
that he took a spoonful of sugar but no cream and
she inwardly shuddered at the idea of drinking
henna-coloured tea. 'There you are.'

'*Grazie.*' He lounged back in his chair with
the cup and saucer, and Jorja noticed that he
stretched his leg as if to ease it. 'Do eat a cake or
two, they look delectable and I am aware that you
ate like a bird at the reception.'

She wanted to beg him not to say that word too
loudly. A stout woman in bright pink was seated
not far away and Jorja felt certain she was the type
to have ears like a bat. Females with dominant
noses always seemed to have ears that rarely
missed a word of other people's conversations,
and Renzo had such a resonant voice that even
his accent couldn't blur his faultless English.
Over the rim of her cup Jorja could see that the
lady in pink had already decided that they were
worth scrutinising.

'A good strong cup of tea,' Renzo said approv-
ingly, and he glanced about him. There was a
tinkle of piano keys as a sandy-haired young man
sat down at the grand piano which stood on a

dais. He started to play, and in keeping with the ambience of the hotel the tune was from a lush musical of yester-year. It stole in and out of the rococo archways and ran its soothing touch along the ends of Jorja's nerves.

She took an éclair which oozed rich cream as she sliced into it. The cream and pastry overlaid by smooth chocolate were as soothing as the *South Pacific* music, and Jorja suddenly felt hungry. She had been too nervous to eat breakfast and had been awake very early in the spare bedroom of Flavia Scott's apartment near Hyde Park. She had stayed several days with Flavia before the wedding, unable to bear the tension at home.

Aunt Beatrice had taken it for granted that Jorja's reserve about the wedding was related to her father's disapproval. 'You should be happy for the child,' she had reproved him. 'Do you want her to end up like those women at the hotel where I've been living? Entirely alone and dependent on the cut-price board and lodging, not to mention the cold cuts for luncheon.'

'Humph!' had been his sole reply. It had been a relief for Jorja to get away to London and she had been happy to accept Flavia's invitation to stay with her. Her apartment was light and modern, with a panoramic view of the park where Jorja had taken walks and pondered the strange turn which her life had taken.

'You are very deep in thought.'

Jorja glanced up from her second cake and felt the usual, deep-centred shock when she met

Renzo's eyes. They were a deep grey, darkly shaded by his lashes and framed by bold, straight brows. She was of the opinion that just like Lucifer in the story of the fallen angel it didn't show in that striking face that Renzo Talmonte was a vengeful devil.

'I've had a lot to think about,' she retorted.

'And none of it in my favour, eh?'

'Hardly.' She dabbed her lips with a serviette. 'I can't imagine what you expect from me, Renzo, but if it's smiles and kisses, then you're in for a disappointment. I've done what you wanted, I've married you, but those vows we made are as empty as my heart.'

'Ah well,' he snapped his fingers, 'I've given up believing that a woman's heart can be touched. You looked an ethereal bride but you are now eating cakes with a down-to-earth appetite.'

She flushed and pushed away her plate. 'It was at your suggestion that I eat them.'

'Of course you must eat them.' He pushed the plate back in front of her. 'Don't be so touchy —don't take so personally everything I say. We shall be arguing day and night at this rate.'

'I'm sure of it.' She turned her profile to him and gave her attention to the pianist, who was now playing a selection of tunes from *The King And I*. 'You took me for a doormat because I stayed at home to take care of my father, but that was my choice. If you think you are going to wipe your feet all over me, Renzo, then think again!'

'Only a fool would allow his feet that kind of

privilege.' Renzo shifted his well-shod foot as he spoke and the movement drew her gaze back to his face, where the faintest of smiles lay at the corner of his lips. 'Won't you pour me some more tea?'

'If you wish.' She poured hot water into the teapot and replenished his cup. 'The woman in the pink hat and dress is watching us as if we're a pair of animals in the zoo.'

'Perhaps she's awaiting the moment when we actually spring at each other's throats.'

'It could happen,' Jorja said, with dangerous sweetness. At least their manner towards each other ruled out the embarrassment of being thought newly-weds. The confetti which had clung to both of them outside the church had been brushed off with equal impatience inside the car. It was only in a farce that a bridegroom drew a handkerchief from his pocket and scattered paper horseshoes and bells all over the floor.

'Do eat that remaining cake, Jorja.' He spoke in a deceptively soft voice.

'I left that one for you, Renzo.' And she looked at him as if hoping he would choke on it.

'I'm reserving my appetite,' he murmured.

'Really?' Her face was a mask of coolness but something in his voice made the ends of her nerves tingle. When they went upstairs to their suite they would be entirely alone; even more alone than they had been in the rectory rose garden. She glanced at the palm of her hand where the thorns had gone into her flesh; the tiny wounds had left no visible scars, and none were needed to remind her of the way Renzo had imposed his will upon her.

Upstairs behind closed doors he had the right to impose his body upon her, and her gaze raced back and forth across his shoulders, then fell to the lean fingers that drummed the edge of the table. She almost jumped out of her skin when he said, quietly and deliberately: 'I think we'll go to our suite.'

'No——' Jorja pushed back her chair and snatched her coat. 'I'm going for a walk!'

'Don't be a little fool——'

But Jorja didn't hear him or care any longer that he might be angry. She ran from the tea lounge, following the flight of her heart from a man she feared. She thrust her arms into the sleeves of her coat as she hastened across the reception hall to the doors which gave access to the esplanade.

It had stopped raining some time ago but the driveway was still damp and the scent of the sea was strong in the air. A breeze blew across her skin and combed through her hair as she turned out of the hotel gates. If she walked quickly she could get ahead of Renzo—he was hampered by his leg if he did follow her—and she rapidly crossed the road to the beachside and made her way down the steps to the shore.

She felt safe here in the open air, among people who were at Sandbourne on holiday, laughing and carefree. Jorja felt so envious of three girls with linked arms, who strolled along beside the sea, with nothing on their minds but plans for enjoyment. After their stroll they would probably head back for their hotel or boarding-house, shower and change for the evening meal, and then go out to dance or see a show at the Queen's Theatre facing the pier.

Sudden tears trembled in Jorja's eyes and she brushed them away before they became a deluge of self-pity. As Renzo had said, she had been given a choice, and she knew full well that had Angelica been given a similar choice by a man she didn't love she would have sacrificed Daddy's happiness rather than her own.

Oh, why couldn't she be like Angelica in ways as well as looks? But right from small girls they had been rather like a pair of apples on the same sprig, one of them with a tiny worm of selfishness at the core, and the strange thing was that most people had always made a pet of Angelica while treating Jorja as if she was more responsible even though she was eighteen months younger than her sister.

When they were thirteen and fifteen years old and Mummy had died, household tasks had fallen naturally to Jorja. Each day when she came home from school she had to set aside her homework in order to help prepare dinner and tidy up. Their home-help, who had been with them during the course of their mother's illness, was already in her sixties and, in order to console her because she grumbled about the amount of housework, Jorja had gradually taken on more of the work until, almost naturally, she slid into the role of housekeeper.

It had been different for Angelica. She had a natural gift for sliding out of responsibility; her role became that of Daddy's consolation. With that wide-eyed expression and false smile of hers she would deplore her own cooking and say that Jorja was the better cook. With a helpless sigh she would announce how clumsy she was with a vacuum cleaner, which in her hands had a habit of knocking chunks out of the furniture.

'I'm the artistic one,' she would laugh, and everybody seemed to believe her, including their father. And it was true that Angelica could play the piano a little, sketch dresses she saw in fashion magazines but never design her own, and she even had the reputation of being the beautiful Norman girl even though Jorja was so much like her to look at.

Because of all these scintillating virtues which Jorja was presumed to lack, there had been no dramatic protest from their father when Angelica announced that she wanted to go to London to train at the Jean Marshall School of Modelling. Daddy had cashed in a number of his National Savings Bonds and with utter assurance that she would succeed as a model Jorja's sister had gone to London, where her natural assumption that she was someone extra-special had soon brought her to the attention of such magazines as *Modiste*, *Bon Marché* and *Exclusive*.

She photographed with ease and supple grace, displaying a built-in seductiveness that could sell the zaniest garment. When she appeared on the cover of *Exclusive*, the Reverend Michael Norman carried the magazine about in his jacket pocket and with a touch of shy pride showed it to his parishioners. 'How delightful,' they said. 'It was always a foregone conclusion that dear Angelica would become famous.'

Jorja was looked upon as the Reverend's right-hand girl. Her virtues were less stunning. She was a good child, and one dear old person had assured her that she would reap her reward in heaven.

Oh lord, no wonder Daddy had been so shocked and upset by what he saw as her betrayal of his trust in her. For years he had been listening to people who took it for granted that Angelica should reap worldly success while Jorja baked pies, polished the rectory furniture, cared for the garden, and always made sure that meetings of the Ladies' Guild were well supplied with tea and cakes.

Jorja's thoughts blended with the insistent sound of the surf, the cry of seagulls, the crunch of pebbly sand beneath her shoes. She noticed that the sky above the sea was a stormy gold, and already promenaders were drifting away to their evening meals.

What did she imagine she was going to do? She had run from the hotel without her handbag so she had no money. Right now as she stood almost alone on the shore she had only the clothes on her back and the sapphire ring on her finger.

She studied the ring in the dusky gold of the dying day; it was worth a considerable amount of money but already the shops were closing and she doubted if she had time to find a jeweller who would give her a loan on the ring. She twisted it round and round on her finger and recalled those nerve-racking moments in church, her voice barely audible as she responded to vows that were meaningless. How could she honour a man who blackmailed her? How could she even relate to such a word as cherish when between Renzo and herself there was none of the breathless yearning of people in love?

The sea breeze had turned to a wind which blew her hair back and forth. A shiver ran through her body and she huddled into the collar of her coat . . . she couldn't stay here, waiting for night to fall. She had to return to Duke's Hotel and try to reason with Renzo. He couldn't be so hard-hearted, so set on revenge that he would cast aside all sense of decency and force her to sleep with him. He was a cultured and gifted man who wrote sweepingly romantic music for films and television drama.

He had to have a soft spot in that armour of his, and with reluctant footsteps Jorja made her way back to the hotel. The foyer was lit up by the chandeliers and she was relieved that Renzo wasn't waiting for her, tall and dark, and leaning slightly on his stick.

There was a lull in activity for most of the guests would be in their rooms, in the midst of their dinner preparations. She climbed the rather grand staircase in preference to the lift, which would be quicker in getting her to the door of Suite 202. She dragged her feet on the carpeted stairs and walked at a snail's pace along the corridor, her heart thumping beneath the soft fabric of her dress and the buttoned-up cashmere of her coat.

There was the door, and there the bell that she must ring. Her finger hovered, then stabbed, and she heard the ringing sound inside the suite. The skin of her face felt cold, and she brushed a nervous hand over her windblown hair. By now her heart felt as if it had lodged in her throat, and she waited, and waited for the door to open.

Perhaps Renzo meant not to open it. Perhaps he meant her to stand here indefinitely, like a naughty child waiting for her punishment to be doled out.

Then the door opened abruptly and he was standing there with a towelling robe loosely tied so Jorja saw the moisture that still clung to his skin. 'Do come in, *signora*.' He made a sweeping gesture with his arm. 'What's a honeymoon suite without a bride?'

Jorja flushed and walked past him into the sitting-room of the suite, where she immediately smelled flowers and saw them in vases in various parts of the large room. The brocade curtains were drawn across the windows and lamps were aglow near armchairs and a deep couch. In a wall mirror straddled by roguish cupids Jorja saw her reflection and was startled by the look she had of being a stranger in from the street, the collar of her coat still up about her face.

After closing the door Renzo had followed her, and she could feel him watching her, waiting for her to speak . . . to explain. At last she dared to look at him and she saw his black hair meshed damply on his forehead, and when she met his eyes they glittered like slithers of steel.

'How dare you run out on me!' There was a chiselled edge to his voice that matched the steel in his eyes. 'I don't care to look a fool in front of other people.'

'I—I just had to get a breath of air.' Her hands clenched inside the pockets of her coat. 'You don't seem to realise what a nerve-racking day this has been for me. I don't know how I've gone through with it.'

'It isn't yet over,' he took a step towards her, 'and you did go through with it, to the extent that you accepted my ring on your finger and signed the register with me. Whether you like it or not, *cara mia*, we are man and wife for better or worse.'

'T-the situation can only get worse,' she said with a rush. 'Don't you see, Renzo, we were never meant to be married. No matter how Angelica has treated you, you love her, a-and it would be so wrong for you and I to—to——'

'Don't stop there.' There was a sarcastic look on his face as he regarded her. 'Don't be coy about what you have in mind, we are both adults and we both know what happens at the end of the wedding day.'

'Oh—damn you!' Jorja backed away from him, for in his bathrobe there was a different look about him . . . it brought to the surface a sensual look which his impeccable suits toned down. Also, without the ebony cane to hand, he seemed a younger man than she had supposed him; a virile man with the male ability to feel desire without love.

'Does this farce have to go any further?' Jorja took another step backwards, stealthily, as if she were backing away from something untamed. 'You've done what you wanted, you've put up a barrier against Angelica in case she tries to come back to you. Isn't it enough?' Do you really need to drag me in any further?'

'My dear girl, you knew what you were getting into, but do be careful in taking yet another step away from me. On a table just behind you there's a vase of yellow tulips and red roses and you are in danger of knocking them to the floor.'

Jorja turned to look and instantly he took advantage of her hesitation and grasped her by the arms. 'You never were a match for me.' His mouth was shaded by a mocking smile. 'You ran from the hotel without your handbag so I had no need to follow you. Without money what else could you do but come back to me?'

'I came back in the hope that we could talk rationally about our marriage.' She tried her hardest to pull free of his hands but they were inescapable, giving her a hint of the strength which his air of breeding and his lameness were inclined to conceal. She looked into his face and his dark good looks seemed devilish to her. 'We don't care about each other, Renzo. I'm not your kind of a girl—I never could be. We're oil and water—we just don't mix.'

'I know exactly the kind of girl you are.' His

eyes raked over her face and hair. 'If you were spared any time at the rectory, then you buried your haughty little nose in romantic novels and gleaned from them the idea that love is from the heart and the soul. An emotion so refined and spiritual as to be close to heaven.'

He paused and his eyes dwelt upon her lips. 'It's about time you faced the truth, *cara mia*. You will only find heaven on earth when you give your body——'

'I—I'd sooner let a truck run over me!' She strained away from him but felt him pulling her to his big warm body that was so bare beneath the bathrobe. 'L-let me go——!'

'Afraid of me, little one, or just being coy?' His face drew near to hers and she felt his warm breath on her skin. 'I find it truly amazing that you grew up side by side with Angelica. You read her letters and they shocked you, but can you really say that you have never once given a thought to having a lover's lips on every part of you?'

'I'm not Angelica.' Jorja's nerves fluttered wildly at his words and the images they evoked. 'Y-you want to impose her upon me so you can pretend—I've just told you, I'd sooner die than give myself to you!'

'My dear young wife, you say the most amusing things.' It seemed that her words had brushed off his skin and left no impression at all. 'I happen to be your husband, and I also happen to know that if I waited for you to give yourself to me, hell itself would freeze over while I waited.'

'I—I wish you in hell.' Jorja spoke with a breathless intensity, saying things she would never have believed she could say, for she was still the girl from the rectory whose inclinations had never been those of Angelica. She was the girl who lifted worms off the pathways rather than see them drown when it rained. It hadn't mattered to her sister if she walked on those puny little creatures who wriggled in despair of ever finding the warm brown earth again.

'Hell is easier to find than heaven,' Renzo murmured against her cheek, the chiselled shape of his lips brushing her skin. 'We have both discovered that, have we not?'

'Yes.' She turned her head to escape his lips but they followed the movement and were suddenly warm against her neck. She shivered with emotions she didn't want to feel, and when he started to unbutton her coat she found herself powerless. He slid the cashmere from her shoulders and it fell to the floor, and when his hands enclosed her waist and she felt herself close against him, her knees went weak as water.

She hunted wildly around in her mind for the words that would penetrate his shield of indifference towards her as a person whose moral rights he was brushing aside as if they meant nothing at all.

'Two sisters,' he murmured, his eyelids heavy across the deep grey irises, 'one so eager to explore the pleasures of life, the other so indifferent. Or did you make yourself that way, Jorja, because you were afraid that deep down inside you might want the same things as Angelica? Shall I prove to you, *amore mio*, that your frosting is only on the surface?'

'All you are proving to me, *signore*, is that you want to fantasise.' As she spoke Jorja could feel the disturbing pressure of his hands through the fabric of her dress. They had moved so they were closer to her breasts, and that petrifying weakness in her knees seemed to be spreading over her, as if the throbbing forces which she felt in his body were sapping the resistance in hers.

'What do you mean by fantasise?' He slid his gaze slowly over her face, taking in the flush that was showing through her fine skin.

'Y-you want to make yourself believe that you're with Angelica.' Jorja was trying desperately to stay cool in the heat of his closeness. She couldn't bear it that her composure was giving way to confusion. Always he was master of the situation; he knew how to turn every move to his advantage. No matter what she said to him, he seemed not to care . . . but there had to be something that would make him care.

'I would like to drop the subject of Angelica.' A crystal hardness had come into his voice. 'Do you hear me?'

'You're very audible—oh!' She broke off with a gasp, for his lips were in the V of her dress, and she strained away from him until her spine ached. He wouldn't make her yield to him, and with every ounce of her will she tried not to feel his lips on her skin, nor the pressure of his muscular body.

'I'm not hurting you, am I?' he breathed warmly into her ear.

'Y-you know exactly what you're doing.' Insidiously her body was being detached from reason ... it wanted these sensations which Renzo was evoking as he moved his lips along the side of her neck. Even as her senses swam, Jorja could think of only one thing ... Renzo was making believe he held Angelica in his arms. His eyelids were heavy over his eyes and he was seeing only what he wanted to see; he was holding and touching her sister.

'Get away from me!' With all her might Jorja thrust at Renzo's shoulders, and as fury rose in her she struck at his face, wanting to hurt him for using her to salve his desire for Angelica.

'I can't bear you to touch me—get away!'

Renzo stared down into her blazing eyes and she saw that the edge of her fingernail had torn his cheek. 'Unbearable, am I, Jorja?'

'Yes.' She spoke fiercely. 'You said you could make me feel like my sister a-and now I do. I feel everything she felt, where you're concerned. We both know why she left you for Stelvio!'

Her words hung between them, and for just an instant Jorja saw a flash of pain in his eyes, shielded almost at once by his lashes. He drew himself away from her and tightened the belt of his robe, and as she watched him Jorja brushed nervously at the sides of her dress.

Renzo moved across the room, towards a table where his case of cigars lay on the polished surface. Now he revealed his limp. It seemed suddenly to affect him and she saw him reach out to grip the back of an armchair, his fingers clenching its support until his knuckles showed white beneath his skin.

'You are right,' he flung over his shoulder. 'I never doubted for a moment why Angelica wanted my brother. We are both men of success, but he doesn't need a stick to walk with.'

In the silence which followed his remark, Renzo struck a light against a cigar, then as the smoke wafted about his dark head, he said curtly:

'You had better start getting ready for dinner —I presume you wish to share that with me?'

'I—I'm not particularly hungry——'

'I am, and I don't intend to eat dinner alone.'

'You know what I want, Renzo.' Jorja hated the imploring note that wouldn't be kept out of her voice.

'Do I?' Smoke eddied about his unreadable face, for he had turned to look at her so she could see that nothing was going to sway him. Never had his features looked more chiselled; never had his brows looked more formidably black above the proud Roman nose.

'If you had an ounce of decency in you, you would let me go home,' Jorja cried across the room. 'I'm not your toy—your object——'

'You are my wife.' He spoke the words distinctly and followed them with a plume of aromatic smoke that drifted towards her. 'You bear my name, and if you dare to make another attempt to run away from me, then I shall go to your pious father and provide him with material for a sermon on adultery. He isn't a very forgiving man, is he, *donna*. I doubt if he could forgive even his favourite daughter for being an adulteress.'

Jorja's hands clenched until her fingernails almost drove into the palms of her hands. 'I think you'd like to do that more than anything else —you'd like to see my sister humiliated because you can't bear it that she humiliated you. You'd like to hate her, wouldn't you, Renzo?'

'As you hate me,' he drawled.

Jorja flung back the hair from her brow. 'It seems I have no option but to stay with you, but you won't break me, Renzo. I don't break as easily as a doll.'

'No?' His eyes slid up and down her blue-clad figure. 'How well that colour suits you, *cara mia*. I married a shrinking violet and find I have a young beauty on my hands—luck of the devil, eh?'

Jorja flushed, for there was no way she could strike out the memory of her skin's reaction to his exploring lips, warmly searching the contours of her collar-bone, wandering down into the V of her blue dress.

The French jersey silk seemed to cling to her with a sudden sensuousness and she turned away from him. 'Nothing you do to me, Renzo, will stop us from being strangers,' she said tensely. 'You aren't someone I would choose for a friend.'

'Do you expect a husband to be a friend?' A note of humour had entered his voice. 'In Latin countries, *donna mia*, men seek their friends among other men.'

'But this is England, *signore*. In this country married couples dare to be friends with each other. The women don't just cook the meals and make the beds, they actually play games as well, and they often win the match.'

'I detect a concealed meaning in your words, Jorja.'

'Do you?'

He laughed softly. 'I might not be your friend, my dear, but it's going to be interesting being your enemy.'

CHAPTER THREE

JORJA drew the comb in long strokes through her hair until it lay smooth on her shoulders, just slightly upcurled. She fitted a tiny cascade of sapphires in each earlobe and regarded herself with dispassionate eyes. Especially the neckline of her dress which fell away softly and revealed her collar-bone . . . where Renzo's lips had searched out sensations she couldn't quite forget.

Her own lips twisted into a smile which didn't banish the gravity from her eyes. She was the original daughter of the rectory who had never been kissed until Renzo pulled her into his arms and kissed her.

The rites of the marriage service had given him the rights of a husband and there seemed nothing she could do to win back her independence. She was here at Sandbourne with a man she feared rather than loved, and this was the eve of their honeymoon.

The iridescent night-blue silk whispered about her figure as she turned from the mirror, caressing her skin with its silken touch. She was tormentingly aware of every sound, every twitch of a nerve, each movement of her body. She longed to be again the composed young woman who had gone about her tasks at the rectory, but it was all behind her and she faced an uncertain future.

As the wife of Renzo Talmonte she would live in a genuine tall Georgian house in Hanson Square, an exclusive area of London, yet within walking distance of the Strand and the Embankment. A long way from Sussex, and further still from Italy. But it seemed that Renzo had most of his business contacts in London, not to mention his musical commitments. In various ways he had taken on the aura of a cosmopolitan, but whenever Jorja looked into his eyes she saw not only their Latin beauty but his Latin obduracy where a woman was concerned.

If deep in his system he longed for Angelica, she was now a woman to be scorned. A woman who had proved to him that she could be any man's, and he was the type of Italian to regard her as *puttana* even if he went on loving her.

'And what am I?' Jorja whispered to herself, her hands pressed against her cheeks.

'Ah, you are ready!' Renzo came in from the smaller bedroom of the big suite which had its own bathroom and balcony. A room of long windows surmounted by carved pelmets and flanked by curtains of oyster brocade. The seats of the chairs matched the curtains, and the bed was of Victorian oak, rich with carving.

'Yes.' She stood very still as he came towards her, his look of sombre elegance in no way affected by his ebony stick. Indoors he managed without it, but he seemed to find it necessary when he was under surveillance by other people.

For some reason Jorja winced when she thought of him stumbling and perhaps falling in front of strangers.

He wore a perfectly cut dinner-suit with a silk-faced collar. There were ebony studs in the ice-white cuffs of his shirt, and a whiff of *Eau Sauvage* on his skin, which was close-shaved except for sideburns that were intensely dark against his lean cheeks.

'When I look at you, Jorja, I feel no regret at taking you away from drudgery.' His eyes moved over her very slowly, then he slid his left hand into his pocket and took from it a jeweller's case. He handed it to her in silence, and she accepted it in silence. Inside lay a sapphire and diamond necklace, the blending of frozen-blue fires making her blink.

'I—I wish you wouldn't do this,' she said at last.

'I do it to please myself,' he retorted, and leaning his stick against a chair he took the fiery necklace from her fingers, walked around her and fastened the gems against her slim, bare neck. 'You will play the part of my wife even if you don't feel it, Jorja. I gave you the full script, remember, when we talked together in the garden of the rectory. And in church this morning you spoke your lines with only a few hesitations —look how everyone was fooled!'

'Not Bruce Clayton.' She fingered the necklace tentatively, as if it might burn her fingertips.

'What did Bruce have to say to you?' Renzo spun her to face him, and once again she became aware of height and authority, and that whiff of masculine cologne on his skin.

'Only kind things,' she murmured. 'He sensed that I was—reluctant.'

'Really?' Renzo's hands tightened on her waist, his fingers pressing through the finely woven silk. 'I value his friendship, *donna*, so don't make me devalue it.'

'What do you mean by that?' She looked at him with suspicion.

'I think you know what I mean, Jorja. When we return to London we shall see Bruce quite often.'

'And you imagine I'm going to behave like Angelica?' Her eyes took fire from the necklace he had placed around her neck, and she wondered if there would ever come a time when he would look at her and not see Angelica. If she would ever look at him and know for certain that he wasn't comparing her to her sister.

'Let me give you fair warning,' he held her with hands and eyes, 'if you ever encourage another man and make a fool of me, then I shall make you sorry you were ever born.'

'Perhaps right this moment I'm already feeling sorry about that,' she retorted. 'I don't really know what you want from me, Renzo, but I can't be bought with jewellery. I'd think more of a flower.'

'Perhaps so.' He stood her away from him and surveyed every aspect of her face and figure, down to the slim-fitting evening shoes that matched the colour of her dress. His eyes lingered on the necklace that played its subtle fire over her skin. 'If the good folk of Duncton could see you now, they would hardly credit their eyes. And the one pleasure you can't deny me is the pleasure of looking at you.'

The shaft in his words was that when he looked at her, he saw someone created in the likeness of the girl he both despised and desired. 'I can do without your flattery, Renzo. I find it two-faced.'

'*Grazie, mia donna*.' He inclined his dark head and retrieved his walking stick. 'It would seem that you find your pleasure in using those soft lips to say hard things. Come, perhaps a glass or two of wine will mellow the atmosphere between us.'

'It would take a vineyard,' she rejoined, and swept out of the suite ahead of him, her first few steps taking her in the direction of the staircase, until she suddenly halted and turned towards the lift. Dammit, why couldn't she be as wholeheartedly selfish as Angelica? Why care that it was difficult for Renzo to walk down a flight of stairs? He might break his neck and she would be rid of him!

As the iron-caged lift lumbered to the ground floor, where the dining-room was situated, Renzo stood looking directly across at her, as if with those mesmeric eyes he was reading her mind and finding things there to amuse him.

Her fingers clenched her filmy handkerchief. He didn't care if she was distant towards him. He liked the challenge of it. It added that pinch of spice which Italians enjoyed.

The lift came to a ponderous stop and Jorja

braced herself for the ordeal of the evening ahead of her. In front of other people it was necessary to appear civilised . . . who among those other diners would believe that the tall, suave-looking man who spoke faultless English and wore faultless clothing was really a devil in disguise? All they saw was his handsome face and his courtesy towards her as they sat down at their table in the spacious dining-room with its Victorian décor.

The tables were arranged at a discreet distance from each other and the napery, cutlery and glassware were shining and perfectly set. Duke's lived up to every expectation, and Jorja thought with a sigh of those long-ago days when it had been but a dream palace in the eyes of two small girls.

So much had changed since those days of lemonade and sand-castles. Her father had been a contented man with a loving wife, but with the loss of his wife he had developed into a man whose faith had hardened towards anyone who believed that heaven could be found on earth. His sole weakness was Angelica, and there was no denying her beauty and charm, even if it concealed a streak of recklessness which took no heed of anyone's feelings except her own.

Jorja opened the large menu-card with a photograph of Duke's on the front of it. She couldn't deny that she felt hungry, for all she had eaten all day were a few pecks of the food Bruce Clayton had insisted she eat, and a couple of éclairs.

'This all looks very good,' Renzo remarked. 'I

am beginning to understand why you wanted to come here, Jorja.'

'Oh,' she smiled slightly, 'it used to intrigue me when I was a small girl, so large and grand, with guests who came and went in big cars. It was the kind of hotel that we, at our boarding-house, spoke about with awe. Royalty stayed here in the old days, and the porters wore a very distinctive livery. Most people who came to stay at Sandbourne sent home a postcard of Duke's.'

'And is it living up to your imagined picture of it?' Renzo quizzed her in a slightly amused way, with something questing in his eyes, as if he were trying to imagine her as she had been at the age of ten.

'It is rather nice,' she admitted, but kept a look of reserve on her face. She wanted to imply that he was included in nothing which gave her an ounce of pleasure. If he was paying a lot for their suite and surroundings, why should she be bothered? Perhaps the only way to pay him back was to make him spend money on her . . . she felt certain the necklace of sapphires and diamonds had cost a small fortune, but it could well be that he had originally bought it for Angelica. The sapphires would also match her eyes.

A waiter came to take their order and she chose buttered sole and broiled mushrooms to start with, going on to breast of duck, broccoli spears, baby carrots and *sauté* potatoes. 'And gravy,' she appealed to the waiter. 'The brown sort, with that lovely rich taste.'

'As you wish, madam.' He made a note of her

request, then turned to Renzo who chose goose pâté to start with, prime roast beef and the same selection of vegetables. 'With the gravy,' he drawled.

With the waiter's departure he quirked a black eyebrow at Jorja. 'Our choice poses a problem, *cara*.'

'The wine,' she murmured.

'Will you share a red with me, or have a *bianco* of your own?'

'Champagne would be nice, Renzo.'

'Has the girl from the rectory a preference in champagne?' he asked drily.

'*Belle Epôque Rosé* has an appealing sound.' Jorja had seen it advertised in one of the stylish magazines for which Angelica posed. There were a pile of them at the rectory because Jorja's sister sent them home knowing that their father liked to enjoy her triumphs in the world of fashion.

'You don't mind a pink variety?'

'Not in the least.' Jorja glanced round casually and sure enough the stout woman who had watched them so intently at tea was again clad in a shade of pink and seated this evening with a thin woman in ale-coloured lace. There wasn't any doubt in Jorja's mind that the two women were finding Renzo and herself of intense interest. Oh well, perhaps they were both widowed and, like her Aunt Beatrice, wiling away their time in hotels. New arrivals would be of interest to them for a few days.

Jorja listened as Renzo discussed the wine list with the wine waiter; they spoke in French and she realised how much more of the world her husband knew. How naïve he must secretly find her, the girl from the rectory as he had called her.

Even when Angelica had first gone to London she had already taken on a knowing air and had managed to make her outfit look stylish. Oh yes, they looked alike but under the skin they had nothing in common.

'How many languages do you speak?' she asked Renzo, when the waiter went to fetch their wine.

'Several.' His smile was enigmatic. 'Are you impressed?'

She shrugged. 'It's no more than I expect and it somehow makes your streak of ruthlessness seem all the more dangerous. You are carrying out a vendetta, aren't you?'

'Am I?' He raised an eyebrow, a man of distinction in his black and white evening wear; a man who could converse in fluent French and hide his true self from everyone.

'You're rather like those men of the Medici times, aren't you, Renzo?' The age-old pride was there in his features, yet as always it was impossible to know what he was thinking as he regarded her from across the circular table for two, where at the centre a single red rose was arranged in a slim vase.

'You think I carry a stiletto up my sleeve?' A smile came and went at the side of his handsome mouth.

'You carry one in your heart,' she rejoined, and her eyes dwelt with a blue gravity on his face. 'I know it's useless to reason with you, you'll do whatever you need to do in order to satisfy your sense of injustice—but what about mine? Don't you have the least stab of conscience where I'm concerned?'

'Don't you have the least bit of gratitude for being rescued from a life of drudgery? Did your father ever thank you, Jorja, for your servitude to him and his stony house of prayer?' Renzo spread his hands in a very Italian way. 'I doubt if he noticed you as a daughter until I came and took you away from him.'

His words were a bitter pill to swallow and Jorja felt choked by them. 'How could you know my feelings, or my father's? We understood each other before you came and interfered in our lives.'

'His life was well served by you.' Renzo's gaze was upon the soft quivering of her underlip. 'You fetched and carried without a murmur, and allowed him to regard your sister as the paragon of the family. You have a foolishly giving heart, *cara*.'

'It's stone where you're concerned.' She firmed her chin and despised those treacherous tears at the backs of her eyes, hot and aching to be released. Oh God, what could be more humiliating than to break down in tears in the dining-room of Duke's!

'*Si*, a stone in your breast.' His eyes made a lazy motion across her figure, where the fine silk showed the shape of her without clinging. 'Believe me, I know what that feels like. Do you imagine I was untouched by pain when my sister-in-law showed me the letters which Stelvio had received from your sister? He should have burned them but I imagine their content was a titillation he couldn't resist. The last thing he should have done was to keep them at home where Monica stood a chance of discovering them.'

Renzo shrugged. 'It would seem that love makes fools of us all—blind fools!'

'All the same,' Jorja bit her lip, as if to punish that quiver he couldn't help noticing, 'I'd done nothing to warrant what you've done to me.'

'You look at me as if I am the Marquis de Sade who has put you in chains with the intention of torturing you, *à la Justine*.'

'I've never read filth,' Jorja said scornfully.

'You read Angelica's letters.'

Jorja felt her skin go ice-white. 'You're pitiless, that's what you are, Renzo.'

'Maybe so.' He shrugged as if her opinion of him didn't worry him unduly. 'Revenge may well be wicked but the impulse is a very natural one.'

'Unnatural in your case,' she retorted. 'You're taking out your spite on me.'

'Ah, but when have I been spiteful to you, *donna*?' His eyes were faintly mocking. 'When I've laid hands upon you, it has been to feel the silkiness of your skin.'

'T-that's what I mean——'

'What do you mean?' He leaned forward and fingered the petals of the flower between them.

'Come, tell me that when I touch you, you feel nothing at all. I think you do, *cara*. I think you are an untried girl of twenty-two, with feelings that want to come alive, so what is so bad that they come alive in my arms?'

'Without any love?' She looked at him in almost a shocked way.

'*Santo Dio*, I find it hard to believe that you are a young woman of this century,' he softly laughed. 'Time must have stood still in Duncton and made of you the last of the virgins.'

This time she flushed to the roots of her fair hair. 'You're like those brutes in the story of the Sabine women,' she breathed.

'How many things I am.' He assumed a look of mock despair. 'Every rogue in the history books except a husband.'

'Some husband!'

'Some wife, which makes us a pair well-matched.'

'As a rabbit and a rattlesnake.'

'A divine comparison, my dear.'

'Don't mention it.' She smiled her sweetest at the waiter who served her sole with mushrooms, which looked so appetising that Jorja could barely wait for their wine to be poured, a Riesling which she hoped wouldn't clash with the *rosé* champagne due to be served with her duck. Oh well, if the rich food and the rare wines made her billious, then she would have the perfect excuse for eluding Renzo's later intentions.

'Wonderful sole,' she murmured. 'It melts in the mouth.'

'I can see that you relish the food,' he drawled.

She ate a delicious piece of mushroom and felt pleased with herself for being able to prod him on a nerve now and again. She sipped wine, buttered crusty knobs of bread, and left only the bones on her plate. 'That was good, madam?' Their waiter gave her an approving look.

'Yes, thank you.' She twisted the stem of her wine glass about in her fingers and felt slightly embarrassed. She had eaten the fish as if she were starving, but Sandbourne was that kind of a place, the air had always been marvellous and she had taken that solitary walk along the foreshore. Oh, that walk and those resolves which Renzo had brushed aside as if they were fluff on his sleeve.

Jorja moved her gaze about the dining-room, noticing how other women were so relaxed and self-assured, as if they never looked inside themselves, nor ever questioned their right to all this grandeur, all this perfectly cooked and perfectly served food. She didn't feel like one of these people, even though her dress was of real silk and her jewels were genuine. She was aware of her own simplicity and it made the huge dining-room seem like a theatre, the other diners so many actors playing parts in a stage production.

A woman laughed and the sound was so artificial that it made Jorja want to run away again, before life with Renzo Talmonte turned her into a shallow creature who lived only for luxury and who paid for it with a body whose feelings were of marble rather than flesh.

'What a very pensive expression you wear, Jorja.'

'I was thinking——'

'Obviously.'

'Do you admire the kind of women in this dining-room?'

'What answer am I supposed to give you?' Something intent had come into his Latin eyes. 'Are you fishing for a compliment, *cara*? Do you want me to compare a rose to a bunch of painted lilies?'

Her eyes widened upon his face, their pupils so expanded that the irises were rings of clearest blue. 'Y-you see it too, don't you?'

'What do I see?'

'The play-acting.'

'Isn't life a stage and people the players? Didn't Shakespeare say so?'

'But don't you see, Renzo, I can never fit into your life. I can never be the mistress of your smart house in London—I'm all wrong for the part you want me to play a-and you must let me go!'

'*Povero me*, are we back to that?' A sudden flash of deadly anger lit his eyes. 'You had six weeks in which to approach your father with the truth but you chose to let him go on living with the deceit. Is that really what you want to live again, being made to feel the drab housekeeper while your sister is constantly adored as the glittering prize of the family?'

Renzo tossed back some wine. 'If you want that, Jorja, then you must be a glutton for punishment!'

Slowly she lowered her gaze and absorbed his words. They held a certain truth, for there had been that six-week interval before the wedding in which she could have told her father . . . everything. Each day she had tried to find the courage, and each night she had lain awake and felt the courage die. She couldn't let him read those letters in which Angelica had described in vivid detail her lovemaking with a man who had a wife and a child. She had made constant references to Stelvio as a married man, and that he owed it to her to discard his wife and child.

Finally, he had done so, and that in itself would have been shock enough for the Reverend Michael, who all his life had preached that constancy was the foundation stone of an abiding marriage.

'Don't cry,' Renzo spoke half-mockingly. 'Not when you have half the men in this room looking at you with such admiration. They'll think me a black-hearted brute.'

'You are, and you won't catch me crying over you.' But a huskiness in her voice was a betrayal of the inner turmoil which she felt. 'I—I can do without your sarcasm, Renzo.'

'Is that what it is?'

'I'm not so country-bred that I don't know when someone's being funny at my expense.' She averted her gaze from him. 'There's a double meaning in everything you say—we have a saying in the country, don't trust a black-browed man.'

'We have a saying in my country, never pluck

a green fig.' His eyes narrowed thoughtfully beneath his black brows. 'Perhaps I should wait until you ripen before I do any plucking.'

Jorja's nerves jarred at his words. 'What do you mean?'

'How green you are that you don't guess what I mean.'

He was wrong, she had guessed and it seemed hardly possible that Renzo would stay his hand and deny himself the full satisfaction of his vendetta. 'You're only playing cat and mouse with me, Renzo, and I don't intend to be taken in by you.'

'Do you imagine I can't resist your charms, Jorja?'

'I doubt if you can resist getting your value from every pound you've spent on me,' she rejoined.

'What a mercenary remark, my dear.'

'I'm not your dear, and you seem to forget that I spent years making the most of a parson's salary. Now and again a parishioner would give us a few eggs or a chicken and it was like manna from heaven.'

'I realise there have been hardships, Jorja.'

'You can't realise.' Her eyes strayed over his impeccable jacket and the gleaming studs in the cuffs of his shirt. 'Even if the wealth ran out in your family there was still the trust fund which you told me about, which enabled you to have a full education. I barely had time to study my schoolwork. My mother died and someone had to keep things from falling apart at the rectory.'

Jorja gave a shrug. 'Not that I'm complaining. I never had my sister's ambitious nature, and I felt it was enough to be needed.'

'Now you no longer feel needed, eh?'

She couldn't read his face, or tell if he was being ironic, and in the pause between them, their waiter wheeled a trolley to the side of the table on which reposed a succulent joint of beef. As the beef was being carved for Renzo, Jorja's duck was served by a boyish-looking waiter whose gaze seemed mesmerised by her necklace. Finally the food was ready on their plates, and Jorja ate her dinner in a thoughtful mood.

Renzo's words about the green fig kept going through her mind. Had he decided not to treat her like a wife? There wasn't a scrap of affection between them, and it seemed to Jorja that to be taken without love was as sordid as being a bought woman.

As she lifted her glass of *rosé* champagne she gave Renzo a surreptitious look. He was eating his meal with a deliberate kind of enjoyment, and he had decided to share the champagne of her choice. How well he fitted into the ambience of Duke's, whose embellishments had sustained their style through the changing decades, the modern world kept firmly outside its windows and doors. It had been designed for men such as Renzo, who had the taste and looks of days gone by.

Jorja was uncertain of herself, and she dismissed his notion that other men in the room were regarding her with admiration. He wasn't dining with Angelica who had always had an immediate effect on those around her, whereas Jorja neither sought nor expected to be the centre of attention.

Renzo's remark seemed like wishful thinking to Jorja. One more sign that he wanted Angelica with him . . . as he had believed her to be, as constant in her ways as she was lovely in her looks.

'We should drink a toast,' he said, raising his own glass. 'Shall we drink to the future, or will you accuse me of being sarcastic?'

She flushed slightly. 'What kind of a future is it going to be, Renzo?'

'What kind would you like it to be, Jorja?'

'I—I don't know—a lot of it is up to you, isn't it?'

'You prefer to be an ornament in my house rather than a possession, eh?'

'At least a—guest.'

'A guest!' The irony in his voice was mirrored by his eyes. 'I think my staff will find it just a trifle odd if the Signora Talmonte behaves as if she is on a visit to me. I think you may have to try and look as if you live with me.'

Jorja took a quick, steadying sip of her champagne. 'Then you do mean to—to regard our marriage as simply a contrivance? You did say, didn't you, Renzo, that it would act as a barrier against Angelica should she—want to come back to you?'

'A *mariage de convenance*, as the French say.' He took a deep swallow of his champagne. 'It would be tantamount to rape if I did anything else, and what could be more pathetic than a lame man chasing a reluctant bride around the bedroom?'

'I—I don't like to hear you use that word——'

'Rape?' he queried, pitching his voice down low.

'No.' Her eyes couldn't quite meet his. 'I—I don't think of you as lame—the weakness in your leg is barely noticeable, and I dare say most people relate your walking stick to your air of distinction.'

He was silent when she said that, and Jorja held her breath. He was surely going to say something with a sting in it, but instead he went on with his dinner, his smooth black head bent to his plate. He was truly an enigma and Jorja decided not to try and fathom his personality. At least he wasn't going to demand that they share a bed . . . after all, she was but the mirror-image of Angelica . . . she was the shadow and not the substance of his desire.

Jorja liked him much better now she didn't have to think of him as a lover.

'Have you left a little room for dessert?' he asked.

She nodded and had vanilla ice-cream topped by a delicious strawberry sauce. He had cheese and biscuits, and Jorja wondered if she could regard him as a sort of guardian. He was very clever and she might improve her education in his company.

When they left the dining-room Jorja's heart felt lighter, and she could hear music drifting along a corridor with marble columns. Their intention had been to sit in the lounge where coffee was being served, but when she heard the music, and the unmistakable shuffle of dancing feet, Jorja caught at Renzo's arm and asked if they could watch the dancing for a while.

He glanced down quizzically at her eager face. 'As you wish, *donna*, but you may not be content just to watch and I can't be your dancing partner.'

'I can't dance either,' she said, but this wasn't strictly true. There had been the occasional hop at Duncton's village hall and as the rector's daughter she had always been involved.

When they walked in where the music was being played, Jorja smiled a little as she compared Duke's ballroom with Duncton's village hall. Brilliant chandeliers hung from the ceiling and there were groups of chairs arranged in elegant arcades all around the room.

'I feel as if time has stood still,' she smiled. 'As if we're Edwardians.'

'But the band is playing a foxtrot,' Renzo said drily, 'and the music is by Jerome Kern, perhaps the most popular writer of songs who ever lived.'

'You know a lot about music, don't you, *signoresco*?' Her mood was so much lighter, and it was hard to believe that she had wanted the rich food and the unaccustomed wine to make her ill. Perhaps the champagne had gone to her head.

'I expect I do.' He raised his hand slightly as a waiter looked into the ballroom to see if a guest required coffee, or perhaps a brandy. The waiter made his discreet way to Renzo's side and took his order for coffees with cognac.

'Napoleon, if you have it.'

'Yes, sir.'

As Jorja sat down in one of the brocade-seated chairs she reflected to herself that she had never seen manners quite like Renzo's, so unstudied and certain. When he sat down in the companion chair she found her gaze resting on his left leg. What did a leg look like after every bone had been so badly broken that the surgeon had wanted to amputate?

Renzo's mother had refused to allow the operation, and quite suddenly Jorja wanted to ask him if his mother was still alive. But it was somehow a personal question and she decided against it.

'What is that tune they're playing?' she asked instead.

'*A Fine Romance*,' he replied, in a dry tone of voice. 'Quite appropriate, wouldn't you say?'

'Is it?' She looked at him in a questioning way.

'Obviously you've never heard the lyrics.' His lips twitched with amusement. 'It's a romance *sans* kisses, in which the boy laments that the girl is cold as yesterday's mashed potatoes and he might as well play bridge with his old maid aunt. The girl won't nestle, nor will she wrestle—in short, the romance hasn't got a chance.'

'Like ours?' Jorja murmured.

'Just like ours—*grazie*.' Renzo took his coffee and cognac from the waiter, and Jorja felt herself being very careful as she took her own. The music died away but the words as quoted by Renzo remained in her mind . . . so curiously apt.

The couples out on the floor returned to their seats, and bursts of conversation and laughter took the place of the music until it struck up again.

'Would you mind, sir, if I danced with the young lady?' a voice enquired.

Jorja came out of her thoughts and saw standing in front of Renzo a young man with athletic shoulders, his fingers at his bow-tie as he met her startled gaze.

Renzo turned deliberately to look at her, and she said quickly: 'I'm afraid I don't dance.'

'But it's quite easy.' The young man smiled coaxingly. 'I'm sure you'd soon pick it up.'

'Do make the attempt, child,' Renzo drawled, and he took her cup and saucer from her hand. 'Go along with you, you don't want to spend the evening sitting with me.'

'But I——'

'I won't take no for an answer.' The young man impetuously reached for her hand and drew her to her feet. 'It's an awfully good band, and the floor is smooth as silk, and everyone can waltz! That's the great thing about Duke's, they allow people to dance in the old-fashioned way.'

'Quite the best way,' Renzo commented wryly.

'Are you sure——?' Jorja was both torn and tempted by the chance to dance, but it seemed unfair to Renzo. It underlined the fact that he couldn't move with ease around that mellow, waxed floor.

'Of course he is.' The young man pulled her away from Renzo, and with a half-laugh she submitted to his persuasion. From the moment his arm slid around her waist she fell into step with him, for she had always enjoyed herself at those village hops. But there she had known everyone and she couldn't help feeling a little shy of this youthful stranger who held her just a little too close to him.

As she pulled slightly away from him, he broke into a grin. 'Why did you make out you couldn't dance?' he asked. 'Was it to spare the feelings of the man friend; I could see he walked with a stick when you came in with him?'

'He happens to be my husband.'

'You're kidding.'

'Why should I be kidding you?'

'He's obviously older than you, and he's foreign.'

'And those two things count against him?'

'I think so.' He spoke with a touch of the arrogance which young men of his stamp learned at their public schools, and with brash eyes he examined her jewellery. 'I bet he's as rich as hell.'

'I didn't marry him for his money.' The ease had gone out of her dancing and she could feel her spine stiffening. She wanted to tell this youth that his self-confidence was overrated and his manners left a lot to be desired.

'Then what do you find so fascinating about him, that machiavellian look?' His smile began to verge on the supercilious.

'You're very curious, aren't you?' Jorja spoke stiffly.

'Who wouldn't be? I've seen your picture on magazine covers and when I saw you sitting in the dining-room I could hardly believe my eyes.'

His words gave Jorja such a jolt that she miss-stepped. 'S-sorry.'

'Don't be.' He spoke insinuatingly. 'Wait till I tell the guys at the rugger club that I've danced with Angelica Norman—though it's a bit of a blow that you have a husband.'

Jorja didn't contradict him, she knew it was the stylish dress and the scintillating jewels that intensified her likeness to Angelica. But it was a mistake which emphasised the fact that neither Renzo nor this young man chose her company because she was simply Jorja, a person in her own right.

'There's something else.' His fingers gripped hers as they circled to the music, and by now Jorja was longing for the waltz to end. 'Is it true that you've appeared in a blue movie? A guy I know reckons he's seen you in one, and according to him it was a real scorcher.'

For brief seconds the sense in the question eluded Jorja, then all at once she felt as if the ballroom and the dancers were reeling around her. Involuntarily, her fingers clenched the shoulder on which her hand rested, and taking this for an invitation the young man pressed his cheek against her hair so the heat of his skin penetrated, along with the musky smell of his after-shave lotion.

These intimacies were alien and unbearable to Jorja and she pulled sharply away from him. She felt desperately shocked by what he had said, assuming her to be Angelica. She wanted to deny that it was remotely possible, but she had read her sister's letters and she was no longer certain that she had ever known the person behind the angelic face of her sister.

'Will you have the next dance with me?'

Jorja realised that the music had stopped, and with a sense of relief quickly pulled free of the arm that still encircled her waist. 'I think not——'

'Is the blue film a secret you're keeping from the rich husband?' A look of insolence had come into the eyes that raked her figure.

'Stay away from me!' Jorja flung off his hand and walked off the dance floor, unknowing how blue and tortured her eyes looked as she went in search of Renzo and couldn't find him.

As she stood there at a loss, the stout woman in pink approached her. 'I expect you are looking for your husband?' She spoke in a pleasant manner but her eyes were all over Jorja, whose hands were twisting and turning the filmy handkerchief which she carried. 'I believe he has gone to the card room, for I saw him going in that direction.'

'Th-thank you for telling me——' Jorja was turning away when a plump hand detained her.

'Do join my friend and me in a drink?'

'You're kind but I—I'm tired. I think I'll go to bed.'

'I must say you look a little peaked. I dare say

you had a long journey to Sandbourne? Your husband is Italian, isn't he?'

'Yes.' Jorja withdrew her arm from the ringed fingers. 'Good night.'

She knew that when the pink lady returned to her chair, she and her friend would avidly discuss the distinguished Italian who came to Duke's bringing with him a wife who was so much younger and far less sophisticated. Let them speculate. The truth was far beyond what they could imagine.

There were several people waiting for the lift so Jorja took the stairs, and it wasn't until she had reached the door of the suite that she realised she hadn't a key. It was in the pocket of Renzo's jacket and he was playing cards . . . then, to her intense relief, the door of the suite opened and a maid came out. 'Oh, good evening, madam.' She stared into the intensity of Jorja's eyes. 'I've turned down the bed.'

'Oh, good.' Jorja hurried into the suite, where corner lamps had been switched on so there was an air of welcome. She sank down on the couch, feeling as if her strength was running out. All she could think of was that it couldn't possibly be true that Angelica had degraded herself by appearing in one of those lurid films which were shown at stag parties for the amusement of a lot of drunken men.

If it was true, how could she do it? Strip bare in front of a camera crew and do unimaginable things with men who meant nothing to her! As shocking as her letters were, she seemed to be in love with Stelvio Talmonte, and those letters had been meant for his eyes alone.

Worn out by her thoughts, Jorja lifted her feet on to the couch and rested her head against one of the cushions. She would rest for a while and summon the strength to get ready for bed. Renzo might play cards for hours . . . how strange a wedding night, she alone with thoughts she could hardly bear, and her husband of ten hours at the card table with strangers.

Her eyes grew heavy and her cheek sank deeper into the silk cushion. Dimly she heard a clock chiming as she fell asleep.

CHAPTER FOUR

SUNLIGHT was bright across the terrace and in through the long windows when Jorja awoke in a large strange bed. She lay there bemused, like someone who had been plunged into a complex dream, then as her mind began to clear she realised where she was but couldn't understand how she came to be there.

She had fallen asleep on the couch in the sitting-room, and she had been fully clothed. Now she was in a four-poster bed and she was undressed.

That was to say she was divested of everything except her slip, the rest of her things had been thrown into a rather careless heap on one of the bedroom chairs. She drew herself into a sitting position and stared at them . . . there was only one way they could have got there, and even as the thought crossed her mind a tall figure loomed between the sunlit terrace windows.

'*Buon giorno.*' He looked every inch the Italian in pale hopsack trousers and a grey shirt striped with maroon, the collar open against his throat. The sun that framed him seemed to intensify his darkness of hair and brow. In every way he seemed a foreign stranger to Jorja rather than the man she had married, who had every right in the world to stroll to the foot of her bed, where he regarded her with the sheet held in front of her.

'I shan't ask if you slept well, *donna*, because I know you did. You were out like a light when I came upstairs at two o'clock, and you hardly stirred when I put you to bed.'

'So it was you——!'

'Who else would it be?' Amusement glinted in his eyes. 'Don't look so affronted, my dear child. At my age I do know what a female looks like, but from the expression on your face a man would think that you had something you wanted to hide from him.'

'Y-you could have woken me——' Jorja could feel herself blushing beneath his amused eyes.

'It would have been a crime to do so. You were sleeping like a baby and when I lifted you, you barely roused—oh, don't look surprised, Jorja. I'm not that much of a lame dog.'

'I know——' She bit her lip. 'Someone told me you'd gone to the card room and I didn't want to disturb you. Luckily the maid was in the suite, turning down the bed. Did you sleep in the smaller room?'

'You know I did.' His eyes dwelt lazily on the virgin pillow beside her own. 'Wasn't that the arrangement? Do you imagine I'd take clandestine advantage of you? I'm not that desperate for your body, appealing as it is.'

Words which evoked images of herself being unclothed by him, his lean fingers unhooking her dress and her lacy bra; undoing the suspenders of her sheer stockings and rolling them down . . .

the intimacies of a lover and they weren't lovers.

'I've ordered breakfast,' he said. 'We'll eat on the terrace.'

'All right.' Her fingers gripped the sheet. 'I'd like to take a shower.'

'By all means.'

He returned to the terrace and once again Jorja was struck by his ability to walk without the aid of a stick when he was alone with her. It seemed as if he had grown used to carrying the ebony stick in public, perhaps to rely on, or because it had become part of his personality. When he laid it aside he seemed to grow younger, more flexible, more noticeably a man of enormous physical impact.

The thought flitted in and out of Jorja's mind that Angelica had not only behaved badly, she had behaved foolishly.

The bathroom adjoining the bedroom was a joy, big and white and with lashings of hot water. Jorja had spent years enduring the bathroom at the rectory, where the water was always tepid and where she had to dry herself rapidly because of the cold draught that blew under the door. There had never been money to spare for improvements, and according to her father it didn't hurt anyone to be a spartan.

It might not hurt, she thought, as she dried herself at Duke's on a large fluffy towel, but it certainly made a change to indulge in a little luxury.

As she dressed herself she couldn't help wondering what her father's reaction would be if he saw her clad in cabin-boy breeches laced just below the knees, topped off by a shirt with soft full sleeves. He seemed to relish photographs of Angelica in such clothes but Jorja doubted if he would approve of the way she looked; he had grown too accustomed to seeing her with an apron over her long-lasting slacks and skirts.

As she stepped on to the terrace and approached the table where breakfast had been laid in a ray of sunlight, Renzo rose to his feet with his meticulous courtesy and drew out a chair for her. Jorja could feel his eyes appraising her outfit as she sat down.

'You look very festive,' he remarked. 'When we've eaten you will show off Sandbourne to me.'

'I'd like that.' She lifted the cover of one of the dishes and the aroma of fried bacon made her appetite quicken. 'It's a lovely morning—shall we walk?'

'If you can be patient with the impediment which makes my step less light than your own?' He lifted another of the food covers and revealed crisply cooked sausages and tomatoes. 'Mmm, smells very appetising.'

Jorja nodded and helped herself to something of each. 'I don't mind your leg, Renzo.'

'Yesterday you implied that you did.' He unfolded the linen serviette in which hot rolls had been wrapped.

'Surely you didn't believe me?' She accepted one of the rolls but avoided his eyes.

'I am not quite certain.' He broke a roll in his

lean fingers and the sunlight flickered on the golden band of his ring . . . the ring which in church Jorja had been instructed to place on his finger.

'Oh, but I wouldn't hold your leg against you,' she protested. 'You made me say—what I did say.'

'Excellent bacon,' he commented. 'Why, because I kissed you, and you have it in your head that kissing has to be sinful in our situation?'

Jorja popped a wedge of buttered roll between her lips and hoped that her look was one of sang-froid. Inwardly he had touched a nerve with his statement. It wasn't just the way she had lived at the rectory which made her the way she was; it was as if she had been born with certain ideals about people, and one by one the people in her life were proving themselves less than ideal.

Although she had known of Angelica's faults, they had seemed forgivable when weighed against her charm . . . a vivacious charm which like a glittering mask concealed the true Angelica.

Her gaze lifted from her plate and she found Renzo looking at her with a certain gravity in his eyes. Did he know everything about Angelica? How shameful if he did? What a blow to his pride if he had seen her performing in one of those films in which every kind of sexual activity was exploited.

Then, as if tuning in to her thoughts, Renzo asked her if she had enjoyed herself at last night's dance.

'Not really.' She poured herself some more

coffee and busied herself with the jar of apricot jam.

'Did the young man try to flirt with you?'

'In a way——'

'There is only one way,' Renzo drawled.

'He——' Jorja took the plunge. 'He mistook me for Angelica!'

'*Santo Dio.*' Renzo's eyes were shadowed by his frown. 'Of a certainty there's a resemblance, perhaps more apparent when you are in evening dress and wearing make-up. Were you upset by his mistake? Did you assure him that you are not Angelica?'

Jorja shook her head. 'This jam is delicious —no, I didn't want to dance with him a second time, so I—I said nothing. What does it matter?'

'You don't think it matters?' His frown was still heavy across his eyes as they searched Jorja's face.

'Not where he's concerned.' Her lips gave a little twist of distaste. 'You know the type, affected public school voice and a condescending manner. And underneath it all a low-class mind.'

This time Renzo elevated an eyebrow. 'You have strong opinions on the subject, Jorja.'

'Not because he mistook me for Angelica,' she hastened to assure Renzo. 'I just happen to think that our public schools can produce a type of snob who is basically good-for-nothing. They're not really educated but the old school tie convinces people that they can run the country.'

'So you found your dancing partner a young boor?'

'I did.' She smiled but stark in her mind was her memory of what he had said in relation to Angelica. 'Would you think me greedy if I ate a banana?'

He selected a banana from the dish of fruit which had been placed on the table with their breakfast. He handed it across to her, then lounged back in his chair and lit one of his thin dark cheroots.

'Yours is a strange, unpredictable country, *donna*, and it never ceases to amaze me that one day it can be so wet and grey, and the following day so sunlit. You were right to suggest that we honeymoon at Sandbourne. The sea from here is like smooth, heavy silk. Take a look!'

Jorja was halfway through her banana, not totally unaware of how Renzo regarded her. She was like the English weather and he couldn't be sure of her . . . he wasn't to know that she could no longer be sure of herself.

'It's an enormous terrace, isn't it?' She pushed back her chair and went to the parapet, which was rounded and overlooked the hotel swimming-pool, the exact shape of a kidney and dazzling blue. Some of the guests swam there lazily; a few had already stretched out on loungers in order to enjoy the sunshine.

How strange life was? It was as if when she was a child of ten her wish to see inside Duke's had been destined to come true. This was genuine warm stone beneath her hands, the laughter that floated up from the pool was real, and there across the terrace the man at the table was more profoundly real than anyone else.

She heard the sudden scrape of his chair as he stood up, then the slight halt in the way he walked as he came and stood beside her. Her hands tightened on the stonework as she felt his tall proximity, every inch of his skin, every sinew and every hair so potently male. His warm, smoky, *Eau Sauvage* smell was becoming familiar to her, as were the fascinating nuances of his voice.

'I prefer to swim in the ocean,' he remarked. 'It's more invigorating.'

Jorja cast a look of surprise at him, and he caught it. 'Do I seem so handicapped to you, young woman?' he demanded.

'Not in the least——'

'When I take you swimming you will find out that in the water I am far from lame.'

'You have a complex about your leg,' Jorja told him. 'I'm sure it hasn't stopped you from doing any of the things you like to do. I expect you still go riding.'

'I keep a couple of horses stabled in a London mews,' he admitted. He lifted his cheroot and drew on it, the smoke sliding out into the ocean-scented air. 'Are you afraid of horses, like your sister?'

'No, I'm not.' Her fingers resentfully gripped the parapet. 'Everyone keeps mixing me up with her . . . as if I'm her shadow instead of an individual with my own likes and dislikes; my own fears and braveries. I begin to wish——'

'That you were not Angelica's sister?'

'Yes.' Jorja gazed towards the sea, a wing of hair screening her profile. 'I—I seem to be living her life instead of my own, and there's a falsity to our marriage that nothing can set right. I'm just the stand-in for the star!'

'You are the Signora Talmonte.' His hand closed upon hers, warm and firm. 'What is she at this very time? The *amante* of my fool brother, who like the majority of men will return to his wife when the excitement of illicit love begins to fade. It does, you know, and when all is said and done, Stelvio is a Roman Catholic and his conscience will drive him first to confession and then back to his family.'

'You think his wife will take him back?' Jorja asked curiously.

'Monica continues to love the fool, and Italian women can be most understanding of the peccadilloes of their men. There is a great deal of the mother in the women of my country, you know.'

'Yet your sister-in-law gave you those letters,' Jorja reminded him.

'Ah, but she was hurt and angry—wouldn't you feel the same? That is,' he gave a low, sardonic laugh, 'if you loved a husband as much as Monica loves hers.'

'You seem to think that a woman should forgive a man,' Jorja said, 'but you don't intend to forgive Angelica, do you?'

'No,' he said grimly. 'I consider that a woman should have self-respect, and her gift of bearing children places her in a special category. When a woman has an affaire she is like a vandal throwing stones in a chapel!'

The intensity in his words made Jorja glance up at him, and his face looked cold and chiselled in contrast to his smouldering eyes. 'Angelica,' he bit out the name, *'il fiore della morte!'*

'Are you wishing her dead?' Jorja exclaimed.

'I am saying that she is like a white flower with dark leaves, which we place on the dead—and, believe me, she is dead where I am concerned.'

Jorja caught her breath at the harshness on his face and in his voice. She found the way he spoke rather fearful, for her life at Duncton hadn't prepared her for people who put so much emotion into their loves and hates.

Life in the vale of Duncton had a pattern to its days which was only disturbed when a harvest failed, or when a prized cow lost her calf.

Or had she lived too innocently in her father's house? Seeing people only as she wanted to see them, the parishioners who had always made such a favourite of her sister, as if they felt easy with the imperfections in her nature which her vivacity and beauty seemed to excuse.

Jorja's hand stirred nervously beneath Renzo's. Without knowing it, had she resented Angelica's popularity? Rapidly Jorja searched her mind but couldn't remember a time when she had ever looked at Angelica and not been as beguiled by her as everybody else. She couldn't believe . . . it was impossible to believe that Renzo wished her sister dead.

'Have I shocked you, Jorja?'

She met his eyes and they still had the sheen of steel between the shadow of his lashes. Her heart gave a curious lurch . . . she remembered when Angelica had brought him to the rectory, and seeing them together for the first time Jorja had been struck by the way they complemented each other. Dante and Beatrice, she had thought, knowing very well that her sister had never liked any sign of a physical handicap, and the handsome Italian, whose engagement ring she wore, walked with the aid of a stick.

Jorja's eyes were reflective. That may have been the only time when instinct had told her that Angelica wasn't to be trusted; that she would always put her desires before the happiness of other people and not care very much if she caused great hurt, or great harm to the person involved.

If Renzo was so deeply bitter, then he had justification for it, but such bitterness proved how much he had cared for Angelica when she had been his *fidanzata*, her hand agleam with a large, square-cut diamond enclosed in golden claws.

Jorja remembered how often her sister had looked at the ring, and when they had been alone in the bedroom they had once shared she had held out her slender hand once again and smiled at the glittering prize on her finger.

'He has heaps of money,' she told Jorja. 'And his family is a very distinguished one in Italy.'

'Do you love him?' Jorja asked her.

'Of course, darling, but not quite in the way you would be in love.'

'Whatever do you mean by that?' Jorja wanted to know.

'Well,' Angelica powdered her perfectly shaped nose, 'as if you'd lay down body and soul for a man. That kind of devotion is all in the past, sweetie. These days a girl has to be practical.'

'Signore Talmonte is in love with you,' Jorja had said, quietly.

'I should hope so!' Angelica had swung round from the vanity-table with the assured grace of the trained model who was always conscious of herself. 'He wasn't easy to land, but I've hooked him right through the heart. He's an attractive creature—apart from that tiresome leg. A pity about that, but it can't be helped. He insists that no more can be done about the leg but I'm not so sure. He can afford the very best of surgeons.'

'I don't think his limp is all that noticeable.' Jorja could remember their conversation with such clarity, there in the bedroom that stayed unchanged after Angelica went to London to make a career. Jorja had decided to let the twin bed remain in the room in case her sister wanted to come home at the weekends, but she came rarely to Duncton after becoming a successful model. She always said she couldn't spare the time, and her visit with Renzo had been but a duty call, so he could be introduced to the Reverend Michael.

When they departed in Renzo's big car, Jorja's father had sat rather glumly in his armchair, as if mulling over the fact that his favourite daughter was on the path to matrimony.

'What do you think of the engagement, Daddy?' Jorja tried to sound casual as she handed him a cup of tea.

'I want my dear Angelica to be happy,' he replied. 'I want her to have whatever will keep her happy, and if she must marry an Italian, at least he's a gentleman.'

An opinion he radically changed on the day Jorja left the rectory to go and be the second-hand bride of Renzo Talmonte.

She gave an involuntary shiver as she thought of that day, and the bleak misery of the train journey to London, staring from the window and seeing nothing but her father's embittered face. It wasn't true that Angelica had a gift for happiness . . . she had instead a gift for hurting people.

'You can't be cold?' Renzo slid an arm about Jorja.

'No—I was thinking——'

'What about?'

'Can't you guess.' She stood unrelaxed within the circle of his arm. 'You're usually good at reading my thoughts.'

'You are thinking that it should be Angelica who shares with me this terrace overlooking the sea.'

'Yes.'

'I have firmly told you, Jorja, that she is out of my life.' His hand suddenly pressed hard against Jorja's body. 'If she came to me and begged on her knees to be taken back, I should kick her out of my way.'

'I—I don't think you would.'

'I tell you I know what I would do.' With his features gone dark he swung Jorja to face him, and his eyes compelled, warned, and threatened. He seemed to personify the inequality of strength between a man and a woman; a strength intensified by his sudden angry passion.

'What do you know of me? What do you know of any man, a girl from a rectory who hasn't a notion how to kiss a man!' He swung her almost brutally close to him and brought his mouth down hard upon her startled lips. His mouth was savage and his angry kisses forced her lips to yield; he pressed himself forcibly against her, as if he had cast aside the restraint he had promised.

'I should have done this last night,' he said savagely. 'Taught you once and for all to be a woman instead of a frigid, puritanical puss of a parson's daughter!'

Between angry words he went on kissing her, lips hard and warm against her eyes, her ears, her throat . . . and in a kind of daze Jorja felt her face and neck bombarded by his mouth. When all at once he stopped kissing her, her mouth was poised beneath his, and her eyes were fixed wide and blue upon his face.

'Enough of a lesson?' he growled.

She hadn't the breath to reply, and he took her by the hand and walked her off the terrace. 'Let's promenade,' he said drily, and as they passed through the sitting-room he picked up his ebony stick, and he was once again the Renzo Talmonte who didn't use his male sensuality to so confuse her.

Was she frigid and puritanical? Yes, she supposed she was, in comparison with Angelica. That was how he had kissed her sister, but driven not by anger. With Angelica in his arms he had been driven by desire.

As the lift lumbered to the foyer, Jorja stood there thoughtfully. Her lips still felt the hard pressure of his mouth; her body knew a little more about the muscular texture of his body.

'Good morning!' a voice called out as they were crossing the foyer. Jorja quickly turned to look and it was the woman whom she thought of as the pink lady, making a majestic and purposeful way towards them. She carried newspapers under her arm, and incredibly enough she was clad in a pink blouse with ruffles and a dusky-pink skirt.

'I must introduce myself.' She spoke directly to Renzo. 'I am Mrs Cartwright and it really is so nice to see people of one's own class at dear old Duke's. Thank goodness this is one hotel which keeps up its standards but the class of clientele has gone down since the days when I used to come to stay here with my dear husband. I met your wife last night, *signore*. I expect the dear child has told you that she was quite at a loss when she couldn't find you, so I took it upon myself to inform her that you had probably gone to the card room. I do hope she found you? As I say, she was looking quite tearful.'

Renzo shot a look at Jorja, then he inclined his dark head. 'We are pleased to know you, *signora*. It was considerate of you to explain my absence to my wife. As you can see, I don't dance but I thought it would be amusing for Jorja to enjoy the orchestra with a partner.'

'I think the dear child is shy, *signore*.' Mrs Cartwright waved a roguish finger at Jorja, who was unable to stop herself from flushing. 'I noticed that she left the dance floor quite soon, and I expect she prefers the company of her husband, just as I did when I was first married.'

The words hung in the air like an announcement, and Jorja felt her flush deepening beneath the woman's gaze. 'It's all right, my dear.' Mrs Cartwright gave an indulgent laugh. 'I shan't say a word to a soul, for I can well remember how I wanted everyone at my honeymoon hotel to believe I was a mature wife rather than a callow bride. It's perfectly natural. Some people are so inquisitive, aren't they?'

'Incurably so.' Renzo spoke in his most sardonic tones. 'I hope you will excuse us, *signora*? We are about to take a stroll beside the sea, this being my first visit to Sandbourne.'

'You will enjoy the resort enormously, *signore*. It's far less spoiled than others I could name —you should take an open-top landau and spare your leg.' Mrs Cartwright squeezed his arm sympathetically. 'I now and again have trouble with my right hip so I know what it feels like to be handicapped.'

Jorja wanted the floor to open and receive her, but Renzo seemed to accept the remark quite casually. 'Enjoy your morning, *signora*. The sun is so beckoning that we could almost be in Sardinia.'

'I expect the two of you are in a world of your own, anyway.'

'Goodbye.' Jorja couldn't get away quickly enough from further remarks of this nature, and she heard Renzo laugh to himself as they stepped into the sunshine.

'Women of Mrs Cartwright's years assume they have a licence to be personal,' he said. 'You must learn not to be quite so sensitive.'

'I had a feeling she had guessed about us,' Jorja said uneasily. 'And she was exaggerating about last night—I certainly wasn't about to burst into tears because I couldn't find you.'

'What a let-down for my ego,' Renzo taunted. 'For the moment the good lady had me believing that my bride was really stricken to find I had not stayed in the ballroom to watch her dancing.'

'You encouraged me to dance,' Jorja reminded him. 'I was quite content to sit and watch, and if you were dying to go to the card room you could have said so. The last thing I want is to be in your way!'

'Don't be petulant, just because that woman said things that made you blush. What of it if she knows we are on our honeymoon? What if she does imagine that I make passionate love to you at every opportunity? Is the thought of my love-making so repellent to you?'

'Yes, knowing what I do know.'

'And what is that, pray?' As they paused at the roadside his gaze followed a gaily decorated landau with a family of four seated inside. The jogging, horse-drawn carriage reminded Jorja of long ago, when she and Angelica in their summer dresses had sat facing their parents in a landau, giggling together and pretending they were a pair of princesses on a state visit.

Oh, if only she could close her eyes and wish it all back; the pair of them children again, unaware of the things that were going to change their lives.

Automatically she crossed the road with Renzo, hoping he wouldn't pursue an answer to his question. 'Which way shall we go?' she quickly asked. 'Towards the town, or in the direction of Ocean Head?'

His eyes flicked her face, then he gestured with his stick to the immense sprawl of cliffs above the ocean, banked into a crescent which seemed to enclose part of the resort. 'Let's get away from the crowds.'

'We have to go down to the pathway.' She pointed out the steps leading down to the beach.

'I think I can manage those without falling on my face,' he said.

'It's just——' Jorja bit her lip. 'I daren't imagine what it must feel like, not having a kneecap. You're used to it, of course.'

'You, also, will get used to it,' he said drily, and he managed the steps with far less effort than she had imagined.

When they reached the path that skirted the beach Jorja saw a game of volley-ball being strenuously played on the beach by a group of young men in swimming briefs. One of them glanced in her direction, staring brazenly until the ball struck him in the chest. 'Who's the dolly-bird?' someone called out.

'Wouldn't you like to know!' The reply came to Jorja across the sands, and she cast a rather agonised look at Renzo and saw only the imperious profile cast in the natural bronze which was several shades of red on the skin of the ball players.

She felt scorched herself by the thought of being pointed out as the model who had lent herself to a scorching blue movie. She imagined it being whispered up and down the corridors of their palatial hotel, so that when she walked into the public rooms with Renzo a chilling silence would greet them. The women would look at her and later on tell each other that they had known all along that she couldn't be as unworldly as she seemed. The men would have in their eyes a look like the one she had endured last night, when she should right away have corrected that young man's assumption that she was Angelica Norman.

Jorja thrust her hands into the pockets of her breeches, the sea breeze blowing her hair about her face and flapping the silky sleeves of her shirt.

Along this stretch the beach grew wilder, huge slabs of prehistoric-looking rock jutting out of the water, giant perches for the seabirds who were flying and fishing in the golden blue light. As a child she had been awed by the great rocks and the way the sea lashed at them when the tide swept in. At tide-turn the waters of Sandbourne were dangerous and markers were put out warning people not to swim . . . Jorja could recall vividly a strange summer day when a pair of swans had ventured from the river estuary where it opened out to the sea and had somehow got stranded out on the rocks and a solitary woman had picked her way among the great slabs, determined that something should be done to help the birds.

The woman had stood out there as the dusk deepened and finally a pair of coastguards had gone out and made her return with them, and something in the scene had made Jorja start to cry. Her mother had said at once that they must return to their hotel, and Jorja never dared to ask about the fate of the swans. She had known, like the woman who had risked a leg on the slippery rocks, that the swans couldn't survive the alien wildness of the sea unless they took wing. Jorja feared that one of the swans had injured a wing and the other one had stayed to die with its mate. She knew that when a swan took a mate it was for always.

She wanted to tell Renzo about that day, but shyness gripped her throat. Any kind of personal talk about those days involved Angelica as well . . . in fact, all they seemed to have in common was her sister. Everything between them revolved around her; she was like a beautiful wraith who haunted them.

'This part of Sandbourne is very picturesque, isn't it?' she said at last, made too aware of him when he was silent, for his silence and the stillness of his profile seemed to indicate the trend of his thoughts. When they walked, Angelica walked beside them. When they talked, she entered the conversation, and Jorja tried to find a topic which might exclude her.

'Does all this—this kind of scenery, give you ideas for a piece of music?' she asked.

'It is rather splendid.' His gaze followed the flight of a seagull, its beak down under the water and emerging with a flash of silvery scales. 'I had not expected Sandbourne to be this wild and lovely.'

'It is unexpected, isn't it?' Jorja took a deep breath of the tangy air. 'I'm glad you like it.'

'Your childhood paradise,' he murmured. 'You recall those days as golden and unclouded, for children have no need to worry, they have only to enjoy the texture of their days and their dreams.'

Jorja gave him a shy look. 'When you talk like that, Renzo, you make me very aware that you're a composer of music.'

'Do I, Jorja?'

'Yes.'

'Are you fond of music?'

'Very much.'

He turned his head to look at her. 'Let me guess, you like "The Blue Danube", possibly the theme from "Romeo and Juliet", and that fey kind of music which is played on an Irish harp.'

Jorja smiled a little. 'You make me sound like a schoolgirl—and you forgot to mention Chopin.'

'Ah yes, Chopin, preferably the Seventh Prelude when you are feeling light-hearted, but definitely the Second Nocturne when you are in a romantic mood.'

'When would I find time to have romantic moods at the rectory?' she said lightly.

'Quite so, *cara*. Now you have all the time in the world, have you not?' He stopped walking and made a bar of his stick so she had to come to a halt. They were alone on the path and only the cries of the birds disturbed the silence as he waited for her answer.

She stood there silently, the half-lowered curve of her lashes hiding her expression from him.

'We could make substance out of our shadow marriage, Jorja.'

Her heart gave one of those frantic leaps which he could induce with a look or a word. 'But last night at dinner—you know what we decided.'

'I know what we said, Jorja, but this morning the sea air is blowing through my mind and it tells me that a man and a girl can't live in the same house and be unaware of each other. I am only human and it's better that we agree to a normal marriage rather than wait for something to happen which you will find—disagreeable.'

Jorja gave him a questioning look, and he laughed briefly to himself. 'Ah, you can't be so innocent—or can you?'

She realised what he meant and her thoughts sped to the way he had kissed her on the terrace of their suite, her body pressed close to the warm force of him so she was made aware of his sensual impulses. He meant her to know that there was a part of him which he couldn't ignore, and she, artless innocent that she was, had supposed that they could discuss it rationally over a dining-table and plan to live as if they were the inmates of a cloister.

The sea wind tossed her hair and moulded the silk shirt against the slim curves of her figure; she felt Renzo's eyes upon the shape of her, his dark lashes intensifying the sensuality of the look he was giving her.

Half-realised images, and long-hidden thoughts filled Jorja's mind in that moment. What was it like, she wondered, to lay naked and possessed in the arms of a man? Did a girl feel the same desperate pleasure and passion as the lover?

Quickly she turned away her gaze unless Renzo read her thoughts. He had experienced what she could only imagine. He was a man and he couldn't know the terrors of a girl who had lived her kind of life. She had never related to the passions of any man, least of all a man who had come into her life as her future brother-in-law. There had been no thought in her head that Renzo Talmonte would ever do more than kiss her hand, as he had kissed it the day they had been introduced by Angelica.

Oh yes, there were terrors . . . all mixed up with wanting to be as different from Angelica as she could get. But when Renzo took her into his arms, she seemed to lose her own identity. When he touched her, he seemed to be moulding her into the shape of Angelica.

'Look at me!'

She slowly raised her face, knowing it to be naked with uncertainty.

'You've gone quite pale,' he mused. 'I shall ask you again what I asked you before, do you find the thought of my lovemaking so repellent?'

'I—don't know.'

'You must know.' His voice had hardened. 'You must feel something when I touch you.'

'Yes.' The word broke from her. 'I can't stop thinking that it's Angelica you want to—hold in your arms. I don't like to think of being used as a substitute for her!'

'Ah, we are back to that again.' He dropped his ebony stick and took hold of Jorja, giving her a shake when she tried to resist him. 'Forget your sister once and for all. Let us both forget her very existence—so!'

The warm exhalation of his breath was against Jorja's face, and then he was kissing her slowly, his lips stroking sensuously over hers. 'Don't do this to me,' she wanted to plead. 'Don't make me like what you're doing to me. . . .'

It was fantastic, unreal, perilous to be locked together like this on a public pathway, but nothing could stop her senses from enjoying this close contact with his vibrant body. His firm muscle and bone had an appeal she couldn't seem to fight, and even as she told herself that this was the man who had threatened her family and swept aside all protest in order to get even with Angelica, her arms climbed about the column of his neck and her lips were soft and willing beneath his.

When he felt her response he pulled her closer than ever, making her feel the throb of sinew and nerve. A deep and penetrating thrill swept Jorja and she clung to him and stopped caring about anything except the touch of his mouth, the feel of his hands, the quickening of desire that was like nothing she had ever felt before. It overrode all other feelings . . . it was excitement and temptation, her awakening to her own body.

She wanted to be his! Nothing else mattered . . . she cast it all aside.

CHAPTER FIVE

RENZO hung the *Do Not Disturb* notice on the door of their suite, then he came into the bedroom and regarded Jorja with a slightly quizzical smile.

She could feel her heart thumping with excitement . . . he and her own feelings made her vulnerable and uncertain of what to do next. She could only stand there and wait for him to make all the moves.

'Do you want to close the curtains?' he asked, for the room was filled with daylight and they were both intensely aware that their instincts were of the night; of the velvety shadows that were more alluring than the bold eye of the sun.

'Yes—all right.' Jorja turned and pulled the cord which swept the curtains together. Right away the room was dim and intimate, and she felt a tremulous, deep-down stirring of her senses, as if the nerves in her body had been tuned in to a single, overwhelming centre of interest.

'That's better, isn't it?' Renzo began to approach her, looming tall and full of intent as he drew near to her. She could see his eyes glinting in the dimness, and she stood before him in helpless surrender to whatever he desired.

She didn't call it love. What she felt was the need and the yearning which she had repressed in order to run the rectory. She had been a pair of hands that cooked and cleaned; a pair of legs that ran errands . . . the in-between part of her had made no demands on the self-effacing person she had been.

Renzo stroked her hair and his fingers pushed their way through the soft mane until they were buried, 'You smell like wheat,' he told her. 'When the sun is hot on the sheaves and they yield to the heat.'

He bent his head and his lips touched her eyelids. He looked into her eyes as he slowly, almost teasingly released each button of her shirt until the silk released her and exposed her bare white shoulders and her breasts in crescents of white lace. He uncovered her breasts, silky skinned and tilting rosy-pink beneath the brush of his mouth.

Jorja quivered deep inside at the provoking touch of his lips on parts of her which had been so secret until now; so concealed beneath high-necked, spinsterish blouses. Only the mirror in the bathroom had been witness to her body, now a man's eyes, smoky-grey, the lids heavy with sensual pleasure, roamed freely over her shape, her skin, as he unzipped and drew off her breeches. From slender thighs her legs tapered to fine-boned ankles and slim feet with straight toes.

And Renzo's hands travelled from her neck downwards, fondling, discovering, with finger-tips that seemed to send a liquid fire racing through her veins.

'I feel such a want of you,' he said, and with his

desirous eyes holding hers he unbuttoned his own shirt, unzipped his own trousers and stood over her, letting the desire build taut and hungry between them. When his strong limbs moulded themselves to hers, Jorja felt the erotic heat and energy of him, the power and passion. His kisses were deep and sensuous, following the delicately sloping line from her nape to her shoulder, a trail of sensation down into her shadowed navel. Her hands of themselves were deep in his dark hair, and the most exquisite agitation had hold of her body, incessant, tremulous thrills arising from portions of her which his intimate lips seemed to know as she had never known them.

Even as her cheeks burned scarlet, her body allowed him to do as he pleased, palpitating in the throes of a pleasure she hadn't dreamed of. Exciting and secret nerves were awakened by his touch so that the entire stem of her body was glowing and deeply stirred. There was something more than sensuality, something so aching and tender and needed that Jorja raised her head from the pillow and kissed his face with soft, gasping, wanting lips.

'*Carita!*' His warm and seeking lips had become more urgent and as their lips fused Jorja felt him between the slender arcs of her legs, caressing, urging, leaving and advancing. Her hands pressed against the muscles of his back, firm as iron overlaid by hot smooth skin. She laid her face against the firm column of his neck . . . a pulsebeat and then a flash of pain radiated to all parts of her body, from the very centre of her to the tips of her fingers and toes. Her fingers clenched, her nails dug into him, and then there was nothing but the tyranny of passion, the clamour of a desire that was overriding, overlapping, her slim body his entire captive.

The bright, hot glow of it blinded her eyes, stilled her mind, swept away everyone but Renzo . . . her lover . . . hers!

His mouth buried Italian words in her neck, his hands caressed and fondled the curve of her shoulders, the softer curve of her breasts, his lips hot and moist against their peaks. His hands slid downwards and held her by the hips to the vibrant motion, the strong pulsations, the delicious churning of their two selves locked into a combat of the senses.

Jorja tossed her head from side to side. Oh God, she loved the warm, powerful, taking and giving body that covered hers. She wanted to die like this . . . or live in the endless wonder of it. She wanted nothing and nobody but Renzo, who was such heaven to hold, there at the innermost core of her.

'You are beautiful,' he whispered. 'So intensely rapturous.'

She clung and gave of herself without restraint, for unleashed was all the hidden need and all the power to feel which her rectory life had suppressed. She was someone she had never known about, and yet she was still herself, exulting in the finding of her own body and what it could feel and achieve in the arms of this man . . . Oh God, his shoulders, his flanks, his heavenly presence deep inside her. She heard and felt the little sounds coming from her throat and her eyes shone with rapture and tears.

'Renzo!' She arched to the glorious feel of him, her mind spinning with stars. 'Oh—Renzo!'

They lay at last in a tangle of legs and arms, her breasts rising and falling against the dark, salty hair of his chest. She felt a hoyden and an angel all in one. She wanted to laugh and cry. She had discovered herself, but in doing so had she fallen desperately in love with her lover?

Or was she being naïve? Was she unable to accept that she could enjoy and participate in the lovemaking without being in love with Renzo?

She studied him from beneath the languorous curve of her lashes, taking in the strong bone-structure, the bold outline of his mouth, the pulse that beat visibly in his throat. Unclad, stripped of his well-made, modern suits, he looked entirely Roman. His skin had a natural depth of colour, for the centuries of sunlight were the natural birthright of Latin men. His skin had a sheen of moisture which intensified its attraction, and his black hair was tousled, strangely endearing in the way it spiked his forehead.

Her stomach contracted to a deep, sweet, lingering ache. He had made a woman of her, dragged her finally and forever out of the big old kitchen at Duncton, out from the oven and the apron, and bared her body and soul in his arms.

At this moment she didn't want to think about the future and what it might bring. Right now he lay there drowsily, sated himself with the desire she had aroused. All thought, all feeling had been channelled into her and left her feeling incandescent and yet melting, like the glimmering of mercury on the surface of water.

Even if the rapture was written on water, it had been throbbingly real while it lasted, intensely climactic and gratifying, and Jorja saw Renzo's lips slacken into a smile, as if he were indulging in pleasant thoughts. His arms tightened about her body. 'Rest for a while,' he murmured.

Her lips moved in a smile against his heart, but she didn't know what to say . . . how to express in words what he had made her feel.

'You are a little quiet, *donna*. Are you—all right?'

'I'm fine.' Her cheeks blazed and he surely must have felt their heat, for the meaning in his words was unmistakable.

'*Santo Dio*, but you were good to take!' His voice was resonant with his sense of satisfaction.

'I—I'm glad.'

'Now you are much more of a woman, eh?'

Her breath caught audibly and he softly laughed. 'This I would say to you in my own language, and more, but you wouldn't understand me. Do I embarrass you, *caramella*?'

'Just a little,' she confessed, her lips tasting softly the salt on his skin, her nostrils tense and susceptible to his maleness.

'I am glad of that.' He sounded very Italian. 'I like it as much as I liked the sweet lack of shame in your body—ah, don't mind that I say this to you. A man wants a lady in public, but in his bed he wants a woman of flesh and fire. This is a natural need in a man so don't be ashamed.'

'I——' Jorja bit down on the residue of bruising which his kisses had caused. 'I don't want to lose your respect.'

'You are my young wife.' He bent his head and slowly kissed her right breast, then her left one, brushing his mouth over the budlike rosiness into which the peaks had softened. 'Every part of you is pretty, *carita*. I would like to eat you, as if you were a candy bursting with cognac.'

She laughed, bemused by what they had drifted into. Her fingers took a tremulous journey down his body, shyly exploring him. His chest heaved against her as he caught his breath, and she closed her eyes against his heart and fondled him. Why not? She longed to know his body as he had known hers. Was it wrong of her? Oh no, it couldn't be wrong, for she could hear him breathing deeply in time with her caresses.

Had he lain like this with Angelica? Had she made herself familiar with his body and felt the pleasure humming inside him like the purring of a tiger? In the warm depths of the honeymoon bed Jorja wanted to cast Angelica out of his system . . . out of his pliant, tawny body once and for all.

She wanted to be his only source of pleasure . . . his hoyden in the privacy of the bedroom.

'So you won't let me relax?' he growled.

'Not on our honeymoon, *signore*.'

Laughing, tense and taut as a tiger, he took her as they lay and with a powerful movement he pulled her above him. His hands stroked up and down her skin as he held her, his eyes emblazened with a passion she was eager to share. She was suddenly and sensitively aware that the intensity of their pleasure had caused his leg to ache and he wouldn't admit to it.

Jorja loved him as ardently as he had loved her, until the chords of his neck were stretched by a cry that thrilled her through and through.

She nestled down and kissed his face, his eyes, his throat. His facial bones beneath her lips felt as good to touch as they were to look upon. The pulse in his throat hammered against her mouth. She wondered if she would have his child, his son, who would have the same striking looks.

The sensitised nerves of her stomach rippled at the thought, and she was careful in her movements as she stretched herself beside him. She had noticed all the fine-drawn scarring of his leg, and that rather shocking absence of a kneecap, and she cuddled close to him and heard the sigh of gratification which stole warmly from his lips.

They slept in unison, and when Jorja awoke to the full darkness of the room their bodies were still in contact, they hadn't moved away from each other while they had been lost in sleep. She breathed in the tangy aroma of him, the scent of a passionate male who had been fully satisfied by their mating.

Jorja smiled to herself in the darkness. It had been so earthy and yet so heavenly, the great mystery of life which in her pursuit of duty she had pushed to the very back of her mind. She had been prepared to be a spinster, who read of love between men and women in the books loaned out by the two old sisters who also sold knitting wool and embroidery silks in their village shop.

The vale of Duncton seemed a thousand miles away, yet in terms of reality it wasn't all that far from Sandbourne. The lights of the village could be seen from the rectory, where it stood a little way back from the winding road, down which she wheeled her bicycle in all the changing seasons. Pedalling through the rain, the winds of March, and the balmy air of midsummer.

Life there had been timeless, with little sign of the changes which took place in the cities. She felt attached to the constancy of it all, and had never rebelled because it seemed that her destiny was centred there.

No one could be more amazed than Jorja to find herself sharing the velvety darkness and the warm intimacy of a bed with a man. It seemed like an erotic dream, but every aspect of it was real and potent, and it was Duncton which had taken on a dreamlike quality. Everything seemed insignificant compared to the overwhelming pleasure of sleeping with Renzo.

She couldn't tell if he was awake. She didn't know if he was thinking of her. She only knew that her life would never be the same again. From now on she would know all about the tyranny of wanting and needing someone, for her body had been very thoroughly tuned in to desire.

Carefully she disengaged herself from Renzo and slid from the bed. She clicked on the rose-shaded lamp because she needed to find the bathroom, and as she left the bedside she picked up her robe from the foot-of-the-bed stool. Strange that she should still feel a little shy of him . . . and yet was it so strange?

This side of their relationship still felt so new and unexpected, so that as she showered she couldn't take her eyes from her own slim body, reflected by the wall mirror. Such overwhelming sensations ought to leave some sign, but on the surface she was still the Jorja she had always been.

But as she twisted and turned beneath the water her skin felt a new kind of response, and exquisite feeling ran up and down her body when she brushed her fingertips over the curves which Renzo had kissed and caressed.

As she watched her mirrored self she saw the colour rise to her cheeks and the pupils of her eyes were so expanded that they had collected into them the gleaming whiteness of the bathroom, making them seem incandescent.

Her heart gave a sudden lurch inside her. She looked so much like Angelica . . . too much like her sister, making her wonder if it was Angelica's face which Renzo had seen when he embraced her and made such ardent and unrelenting love to her. Was it a fantasy figure who had lit such cascades of desire in his body?

Tears sprang emotionally into Jorja's eyes, spilling with all the new hot feeling she had started to experience. Even if Angelica still plagued the heart out of Renzo, there was no going back to their former relationship. She had given and he had taken and everything was changed between them. Even if there was a little pain, every inch of her was glowing with an awareness of life.

She sponged away her tears and slid her body into the ice-blue satin robe, liquid-soft over her skin. She ran a comb through her tousled hair, again and again until it was smooth as silk. Now she looked outwardly composed and a little less like Angelica, even if she had learned that she and her sister were more akin in their sensuality than she had ever dreamed.

When Jorja returned to the bedroom she found Renzo speaking on the telephone, requesting that dinner be brought to their suite. With his eyes fixed upon her, a brazen figure in the lamplight, he ordered sweetbread pâté and toast, beef in Sauce Diable, *sauté* potatoes, broccoli spears and baby carrots. Fruit and brandy ice-cream for dessert, and a bottle of *Belle Epôque*. And they would also have coffee with cognac, a selection of fondants and a box of Caliph cigars.

'Grazie!'

He cradled the phone and came across the room to Jorja, who stood in front of the windows, a blue and gold figure who watched him with a slightly wondering smile. Apart from his leg he was splendidly built, and the deep natural tawniness of his skin made her want to reach out and touch him . . . pet him, as if he were a tiger who wouldn't bite her, at least.

'You look,' he gazed down at her, 'so untouched.'

'You look,' she smiled, 'like a pagan statue.'

'A statue of whom?' He quirked a black eyebrow.

'Adonis.'

'The god of love, eh?'

'At least the god of lovemaking,' she amended.

He held her blue gaze intently with his deep-grey eyes, so darkly lashed, so thrilling her when she had seen them glow and burn with passion.

'No regrets?' he murmured.

She shook her head, not really trusting her voice. She wouldn't speak of love because in their situation it would spoil what they had made of the marriage he had forced upon her. She would forget about love and have in its place a luxury of the senses, for their sensuality was like a warmth between them, an emanation from his skin to hers, penetrating the satin folds of her robe.

He placed his hands on her waist and drew her slowly to his naked body, holding her against him in the ice-blue satin. 'I want to give you pearls to match your skin,' he said. 'I want to give you rubies to match your lips. Diamonds are too hard and brilliant to suit you, and sapphires are somehow sinister. What was I thinking of?'

He had been thinking of Angelica, as Jorja well knew, and she said quietly: 'Give me flowers, Renzo, I much prefer them.'

'Ah, but flowers fade too soon, and I want to see you wearing pearls and rubies. You are, you know, more beautiful than I had realised.'

'It's only gratitude that makes you think so,' she rejoined.

'Gratitude?' He frowned slightly and his hands pressed into her.

'For—today.'

'For giving yourself to me?'

'Yes.'

'I'm not a callow boy, Jorja, who flatters for sensual favours.'

'Oh, you're far from being a boy.' A smile hovered at the edge of her mouth. 'You're so utterly a man that I—I'm grateful you think I'm enough of a woman—living as I have lived in a country rectory, someone who became a stranger to a cuddle and a kiss after my mother died.'

There was a moment of acute silence, and then with a rather incoherent murmur Renzo lowered his head and kissed her mouth with a succession of sweetly piercing kisses. '*Dio mio*, how did you stay beautiful and generous in that house of stone? It should have warped you but instead you are soft and ardent flesh that drives my mind out of my skull.

'Girl,' he pushed her away from him, 'keep your distance or you and I will be making breakfast of our dinner.'

'Now that,' her smile was shaking on her mouth, 'is what I call flattery.'

His grey eyes raked her from head to toe. 'You look a virgin again, and I think I shall take a very cold shower.'

As he strode into the bathroom, Jorja laughed breathlessly to herself. Please God, let nothing break the spell that was binding them, even if its coils were the silky hot ones of sensual desire. He had made her come alive to the very centre of herself, and she wanted never again to fall asleep without his warm and virile presence beside her. Wanted this despite her realisation that there was no true stability to their relationship and that it wouldn't take much to tear them apart. Hadn't he said himself that when the excitement started to fade for Stelvio, he would leave Angelica and return to his family?

It was a train of thought which Jorja didn't want to follow and she went to the four-poster bed, dragged the tumult of sheets and covers to the floor and spent the next ten minutes producing order out of chaos.

That was better, now the bed looked as if it hadn't been disturbed since the maid had seen to it that morning. She had smoothed the top cover so that hardly a crease could be seen.

She was awaiting Renzo in the sitting-room when the waiter came with the trolley and carried in their dinner, which gave off a mouth-watering aroma. He arranged a table between the windows, and brought in the silver bucket with the champagne up to its neck in ice. Next came the stemmed glasses, the fondants arranged like a bouquet, and the cigars in a box with a picture of a desert rider on the lid.

The waiter's discreet face showed not a sign of what he might be thinking, but Jorja felt as if it must show that she had spent hours in the vigorous arms of the man who now sauntered into the room, clad in dark cashmere, corded around the middle rather like the robe of a monk.

'Darling,' Jorja longed to tease him, 'who do you think you are kidding?'

'Excellent.' He rubbed his hands together as he surveyed the table. 'I'm ravenous for my dinner.'

'I think you will find everything to your satisfaction, sir.' For the briefest of moments the waiter's eyes were on Jorja, then he had bowed himself out of the suite and they were alone again.

'Come, let us eat, drink and be merry.' Renzo uncorked the *Belle Epôque* and there was a fizz of bubbles as he filled the glasses with the *rosé* champagne. He sat down facing her and raised his glass towards her. She obligingly clincked it with hers and they drank in unison.

'Delicious,' she murmured.

'Ah yes, delicious.' He smiled directly into her eyes. 'You made the bed, I noticed.'

'I should think so—it looked like the Normandy landing.'

'What would you know of that?' He spread the toast generously with the pâté and handed her the first helping. 'You weren't thought of, let alone born.'

'My father was there.' The sweetbread pâté had a subtle taste of cognac, delectable followed by a swallow of champagne. 'You will think of him as some kind of an ogre, but I remember him as he was when my mother was alive. He adored her.'

Renzo's white teeth crunched his laden toast,

and his eyes looked into the wistful blue of Jorja's. 'If she looked like you——'

'I think he valued her for more than her looks.' Jorja spoke with a touch of sadness. 'She was kind and full of fun and gaiety. They loved each other dearly, and Daddy was never the same —afterwards. I still remember every detail of her burial. The way I held on to Daddy's arm so fiercely, in case he leapt down that deep hole in the ground.'

Jorja didn't tell Renzo that as they had walked back to the rectory it had been Angelica to whom her father had clung. She had always known that he preferred her sister, for there would always be a certain look in Angelica's eyes, something in the way she smiled and moved, that attracted men. Aunt Beatrice referred to it as a touch of Eve.

'Don't look sad.' Renzo leaned forward and added champagne to her glass. 'Don't let us think of anyone but ourselves, for that is the privilege of two people on their honeymoon. They exist for each other.'

'Are you happy, Renzo?' She sipped champagne and wondered what his inner feelings were. Had she touched his heart just a little, or was his pleasure only on the surface, related only to the enjoyment which his body had found in conjunction with hers? Was that all he wanted from her? Was that all he would ever ask of her, the thrill of desire?

'Surely I look a man who has been made happy?' His eyes dwelt boldly on her face. 'Now when we run into the lady in pink you'll have every reason to blush——' He broke off and laughed at the look on Jorja's face. 'I must agree with her regarding the standards of Duke's, they are worth five stars. I might add a sixth for the comfort and spaciousness of their beds, and if ours did take on aspects of the Normandy landing, then it was a beach well worth the capture.'

Jorja felt herself colouring beneath his amused gaze. 'I know what you're thinking, Renzo, but I couldn't allow the maid to see that battlefield. She'd assume—one of two things.'

'That I had taken you by force, or that you had taken me?'

'I had something like that in mind.'

'I don't mind if the hotel maids gossip about my prowess,' he smiled, tucking into his beef and vegetables as if building up his stamina for some more lovemaking.

The thought, the expectation tickled like a feather at the base of Jorja's spine and she could feel herself wanting to give a little wriggle as the sensation crept higher and higher. 'Oh——' She gave a gasp and reached for her champagne, cooling herself with a deep swallow. She half suspected what had occurred and the wonderment of it was in her eyes as they dwelt on the man who without touching her could so thrill her.

'You have the largest eyes I've ever looked into,' he told her.

Which couldn't be quite true, and as the wraith of Angelica seemed to shift from among the shadows, Jorja broke into chatter, reaching into the air for anything that would cast her sister out of the atmosphere.

Music . . . yes, music was a safe topic of conversation.

'Do you compose the musical score when a film's completed, or do you work with Bruce—Mr Clayton—during the actual making?'

'Do call him Bruce.' Renzo gave her a slightly veiled look. 'After all, he gave you away to me—evocative term, isn't it?'

'I'd like to talk about your work, Renzo, or don't you want me to show an interest?' She felt her smile fading as she met his eyes and saw their veiled expression. 'Am I only part of your—bedroom?'

'Is there a better place for participation?' he asked.

Jorja carried a spoonful of brandy ice-cream to her lips, but something inside her had cooled before she swallowed it. The lovemaking was over, she reminded herself. It was time to remember the cruel tactics he had used in order to carry out his vendetta, and all at once those ardent hours in his arms took on a reality which jolted her to her senses.

He didn't regard her as anything more than a wife he could take or leave alone, and it was ridiculous of her to want to have a share in his ambitions and his problems. Only a man in love invited a woman to participate in all aspects of his life . . . the woman with whom he took his pleasure was meant to share only his bed.

She forced the ice-cream between her lips and

swallowed it with difficulty. She wasn't asking him to be in love with her, but she had hoped to be a little more than a body whose responses had been so eager that he might get the idea that she was in love with him. She couldn't abide the thought . . . her pride wouldn't let her.

'I thought it would pass the time to discuss what you do for a living.' She heard the note of hostility in her voice and made no attempt to soften it. 'It might get boring for both of us, if we only communicate in bed.'

In a long moment of silence Renzo stared across at her, then he laid down his dessert spoon and his eyes had a steely glint in his dark face. They were as she had seen them that day at Duncton, when he had made her read the letters which had revealed a side to Angelica which had so shocked her. She could remember vividly the way he had watched her, his eyes cold and yet burning beneath the blackness of his brows.

Then he had been almost a stranger to her. She hadn't been acquainted with his warm and pliant body. She hadn't felt the thrill of his lips as they wandered over her skin and found ways to pleasure her that right now made her tingle and ache for a renewal of the delicious onslaught of feeling.

Her body wanted him even as her mind rebelled against the enslavement of desire. She wanted him in all his naked power even as she told herself that she wouldn't be a slave to that side of their life. 'It is the only sort of communication you want.' Her voice had grown defiant.

'You wouldn't want to discuss your career with your harlot.'

The awful word hung in the air . . . then she shrank nervously as Renzo surged to his feet and came round the table to her. He towered over her and she felt certain he was going to do something violent . . . grab her, perhaps, and shake her until her teeth rattled.

'How dare you speak in such a way!' He seemed barely in control of his anger, something smouldering in his eyes that made Jorja wonder if he had shared a scene like this with Angelica.

'Do you think I will tolerate such insolence?' he demanded. 'At no time in your life have you spoken like that to anyone, so don't presume to speak like it to me!'

Nerves fluttered in Jorja's underlip, for she had provoked a reaction which alarmed her and made her feel as helpless and vulnerable as she had been in the rectory garden, when he had drawn the rose thorns from her hand, unable to prevent the cure from being as painful as the assault.

'*Grande Dio*, what do I make of you?' He reached out a hand, but she shrank a little further from him, like a young cat uncertain of the owner's mood.

'What is this, Jorja?' He searched her eyes. 'Regret, after all?'

She felt almost tempted to agree with him. Her feelings were so confused that perhaps she did regret the intimacy which had led to the resentful emotions they were sharing right now. When two people kept a distance between them it was easier not to be hurt by painful truths.

She tried to control the tremor in her lips. 'I'm still the girl from the rectory,' she agreed. 'A lot has happened to me in a short time and our kind of marriage isn't easy for me to—to cope with.'

'Do you imagine that I am finding it easy?' he asked her.

Jorja bit back the obvious reply to his question, and he reached for his box of cigars and impatiently slit the seals. He selected one of the thin dark cigars and bit the end with his teeth; he raked in his pocket for his lighter and when the flame was applied and the smoke eddying he returned his attention to Jorja.

'There is an old saying, when the kissing stops, the talking starts. *Basta*, if you are not going to finish your ice-cream, then do stop fiddling with it. Come to the couch and pour the coffee and cognac.'

Jorja did as he ordered and when the coffee was poured and the dark gold cognac added, she sat down but kept space between them. It rankled her that it was Angelica who had come between them. Though she was miles away in a bodily sense, she was here in the room with them. The very roots of their relationship were entangled with her, for there would have been no marriage, no honeymoon, if it had been in Angelica's nature to be faithful.

Jorja knew that Renzo wouldn't have looked at another woman if her sister hadn't betrayed him. Jorja was informed by her instincts that he was the type of man to love deep down in his bones, where it would blend into the marrow of him.

She drank coffee in an effort to wash down the tears that were clumped in her throat.

'You must eat some fondants.' Renzo picked up the dish and held it out to her. 'They look very inviting—come! To please me.'

She took one and laid it in the saucer of her coffee cup. If she tried to eat the sweet she would probably choke on it.

Oh God, she was feeling as dramatic as a character out of *East Lynne*. Angelica used to mock her for reading the book, one of many old classics on the book shelves at the village library. 'You'll ruin your eyes, and get ridiculous ideas about love,' she used to say. 'You'll finish up wearing glasses, and then you'll really look like the old maid of the house.'

In that instant, in the very midst of Jorja's meditations, Renzo made a move that brought him closer to her on the couch. But such was her nervousness, such were her thoughts, that she instinctively moved as if to avoid contact with him.

It was done before she could retract. Done before she could mend the damage, and she felt an inward shock at her own action, not unlike a jolt from a dangerous current.

'So that's the way of things?' he said, grimly. 'You are Miss Frigid again—always supposing that I am going to accept a nicely frozen wife after enjoyable hours with a thawed out one!'

Jorja knew what he meant, and there would be

no stopping him if he carried her to bed in a mood of cold rage. He was powerful enough to achieve his desires even if she struggled like mad, and she knew she would struggle against passion used as a punishment.

'I—I don't want to quarrel with you——' They seemed again as they had been in the rectory garden, his eyes filled with vengeful intent. 'All I want is to be treated as a—a person.'

'And all day in bed I didn't treat you like one?' he asked sarcastically.

'I'm talking about now—out of bed.' She spoke defensively, for she could tell from the set of his features that he wasn't going to listen to her with sympathy. 'All you want from me is the shape and the look of me, and you know it! You don't mind paying attention to my hair, or my eyes, or anything else on the outside, but you aren't interested in what I think or feel as a person.'

Silently he studied her through the smoke of his cigar, his eyes narrowed to silvery slits. 'Many women, my dear girl, are content to be admired for their looks, and the way they respond to a man. You are right, Jorja, for me your looks and your responses do suffice, and I am not about to beg you for your body. I shall take it and enjoy it whenever I feel disposed.'

'Whether I want you or not?' The words leapt from her lips of their own free will, and because of what he had said to her, she didn't care. He had laid it on the line that all the lovemaking had not given him a change of heart . . . she was still the sister of Angelica, whom he had married because she had the shape and the look that could stir him to passion and pleasure.

The thought made her burn. She wanted to throw the remainder of her coffee full in his face.

'I can only be hurt once for not being wanted by a woman.' He rose to his feet, his cigar clenched between his hard white teeth. 'Enjoy the rest of the evening in the peace of your own company, my dear wife. I think I shall go and find more congenial company at the card table downstairs.'

'I prefer to be alone,' Jorja said, and at that moment she meant it. As he walked away with the slight halt which usually moved her, she felt temper boiling up in her. 'I hate your arrogance —you can go and play cards with the Devil for all I care!'

He turned briefly at the dressing-room door to look at her. 'I wouldn't trust the love of a Norman girl, so your hatred is fine with me.'

The door closed behind him, and Jorja sat there in the silence, feeling as if there were crystals in her eyes. On the way to Duke's he had said that love was inseparable from hate, and Jorja realised how much truth there was in the statement. The two emotions were like profiles on a coin and at any given time one or the other could reveal itself.

Well, she wouldn't be sitting here when he passed her by to go and play cards. With a rustling of her satin robe Jorja rose to her feet and walked out to the terrace, where she leaned against the stone parapet and felt the sea wind ruffling her hair. She wasn't aware that the crystals had melted in her eyes until she felt a wetness on her cheeks.

'I can only be hurt once by a woman,' he had said.

'I can only be hurt by Angelica,' he had implied.

Jorja scrubbed away her tears but she could do nothing about the feelings from which they had stemmed.

CHAPTER SIX

BEFORE Renzo left for the card room he came out to where Jorja stood and flung a coat around her shoulders. 'You have quite a temper on the quiet.' He gazed at her rather searchingly in the light flooding upward from the hotel gardens. 'Don't stay out here all night, will you?'

'Would it matter if I did?' She spoke off-handedly.

'What in the name of heaven started all this?' His hands clamped her shoulders. 'One minute you were sweet as wine, the next you were calling yourself my harlot.'

'I'm something of the sort.' She fixed her gaze upon the starlight beyond his shoulder. 'Because we stood in front of a priest doesn't alter the reasons for our marriage.'

'Reasons?' He gave her a slight shake. 'I will give you only one that matters, you enjoyed every moment in my arms and it's absurd of you to feel some kind of puritanical guilt. We are man and wife. We are entitled to share a bed. And despite what you may in your innocence believe, it isn't every woman who can achieve the kind of satisfaction which you achieved with me. Relish your body!'

'As you do, I suppose?'

'As I do.' Vigorously he pulled her to him and

brought his mouth down hard upon hers. 'Do you still want me to go and play cards with the Devil, or shall I stay and make love to you?'

It was the word love that stabbed her. If only it was love that he felt instead of a desire he could switch on just by looking at her, the mirror in which he could imagine himself with Angelica.

Jorja pulled away from him and it was her answer to his question. In the upflung light his face looked darkly dangerous, as if he might sweep her up in his arms and do as he wanted with her. She tensed, and she didn't know if she felt relief or chagrin when he turned on his heel and left her alone on the terrace.

She stood there for ages, the things they had said to each other sifting through her mind. There was no denying that her senses leapt when she thought of him in a physical way. There was a tactile strength to his hands which made her feel weak when she imagined them stroking her body, pausing with a subtle awareness of where she wanted him to linger.

Like the proud little fool he had called her, she had sent him away. Hurt little idiot that she was she couldn't bear him to believe that like Angelica she couldn't be trusted with a man's feelings.

She hugged the coat around her and wished it was Renzo's arms, enfolding, tightening, pulling her so close to him that she shared the vibrancy of his body. Music from the hotel ballroom drifted on the night air, and she felt desperately moved by the romanticism of it.

Did she love Renzo, or had she fallen for his sex

appeal? She was so hopelessly inexperienced in such matters, and she wondered if she had felt his attraction when Angelica had brought him to the rectory. She had noticed how handsome he was, and she had seen for herself that he was dazzled by her sister. It had been written all over him, and Jorja couldn't believe that he would be indifferent if Angelica came back into his life.

He wouldn't kick her out of it, as he had sworn he would. No one could do that to someone they loved . . . that was the tyranny of love, and Jorja faced it as she stood alone on the terrace and felt the tangy night air stroking her face and hair.

It wouldn't be wise of her to be in love with Renzo because she would have to live in fear of Angelica, who could smile into a man's eyes and make him forget everything but the lure of her personality.

When the drifting music grew too impossible to bear, Jorja went indoors. The waiter had left the fondants on the coffee table, so she picked up the dish and took them to bed with her . . . a compensation, she realised, for the richer sweetness of Renzo's kisses.

There were magazines at the bedside and she flicked over the glossy pages, chewing a delicious concoction of strawberry cream, half afraid that she would turn a page and find her sister smiling up at her, clad in something outrageously chic. Had she always secretly known that there was no escape from Angelica? That something in their genes, which had made them outwardly alike, would attract them to the same man?

Their difference lay in the intensity of their inward nature. Jorja had always breathed deeper of the roses, and idled to watch the wild birds when they flew to the stone table in the garden, where she scattered breadcrumbs and peanut kernels, not to mention the Sunday treat of raisins and sultanas filched from the jar before she started to bake the teatime cake.

With a sigh Jorja slid down in the big bed and flung her arm across the cool surface of the adjacent pillow. No matter how often she told herself that she could bear Renzo's love for Angelica, still she was left with the desolate feeling that like a bird in the garden she was pecking at crumbs while her sister treated with indifference the feast she could have shared with Renzo.

Jorja knew that her own heart was warmer, her sense of loyalty far more constant, but that was the way of love. For some reason it took no heed of virtues but often flew to the tree which would be barren in winter and bear no fruit to stave off the cold and biting wind.

Wanting an escape from her restless thoughts Jorja switched off the lamp, burrowed down in the bedcovers and tried not to care that she was alone. She had said defiantly that she wanted to be alone, but it wasn't true. Here in the darkness she wanted to be held in Renzo's arms. She wanted his warm breath against her skin, his warm and seeking touch against her body.

Her toes curled into the bottom sheet, and inexorably the desire for him spread all over her. She rolled on to her face, stifling a moan of sheer loneliness. She had brought this on herself and now she had to endure the misery of it. What was a bit of pride compared to the delicious thrill of surrender . . . right now she would exchange every foolish word for the tumultuous fun and pleasure of being with Renzo.

If now and again at Duncton she had paused to wonder about body contact between a man and a woman, she had certainly never dreamed that it could be so profound; two people in communion with something beyond themselves . . . the life force, perhaps, igniting a glow of the soul as well as a joyous satisfaction of the body.

'My luve's like a red, red rose,' Robert Burns had written, so much more simple and direct than other terms she had come across in other books.

Such a communion with Renzo was worth a little heartache. Perhaps even a lot, for there was no seeing into the future and what might happen to their marriage if Angelica came back into his life.

There in the lonely vastness of the four-poster Jorja willed Renzo to come to her. She wanted to wrap her arms around him, here in the warmth she had made for him. She felt a yearning for his lips on hers, desirous and urgent.

She kept whispering his name, and fell asleep with his name on her lips. She awoke some time later and was instantly aware of him beside her. She smiled to herself and turned towards the length and bareness of him. 'Renzo?' She touched him until he stirred. 'Renzo?'

'What is it, *carita*?' He sounded sleep-bemused.

'Make love to me,' she breathed into his ear.

His warm hands found her and brushed away the silken barrier of her nightdress. She quivered deep down. Every portion of her was longing to be his. She clung to him, her lips parting as he stroked the sensitive peaks of her breasts.

'So now you want my attentions?' he murmured.

'Yes.' Her voice was husky with desire, the feel of his body was unbearably exciting, tantalising her with its firm and pliant touch. 'I was being silly—this is all that matters, and you were right to call me a little fool. Oh Renzo, I do want you!'

'Do you, *donna mia*?' He trailed his lips across her throat. 'Tell me how you want me?'

'Y-you know.'

'I want you to tell me.'

'I-in words?'

'Or mime.' He was laughing softly at her, shades of threat in his mood, letting her know that he was a Latin male who made people pay when they crossed him.

'You can be cruel when you like, Renzo.' Her lips brushed his hard chin, softly swollen with the urges of her body. 'I—I was a good girl—a nice girl——'

'Hush.' His lips closed sensuously over hers and his warm body pinned her to the bed. 'My beautiful prisoner. My golden girl. My. . . .'

There the talking stopped and the kissing grew more intense. Jorja lay besieged by his passion and her own, but in and out of her mind floated a question that none of the mounting pleasure could take away. Had he been on the verge of saying . . . Angelica?

Even as Jorja felt the ultimate of physical contact with Renzo, she had a conviction he had been about to speak her sister's name. The magazine writers always referred to Angelica as the golden girl, so who else could he have meant?

'Are you having forty winks?' His voice broke in amusedly on her silence.

'No.' She lay clasped to his heart, which still made a soft thunder beneath her cheek. She listened to the sound and it was like a continuation of the intimacy, a thudding of his blood through the very nerve centre of his emotions. She lay on the outside of his heart and had a mental image of her sister locked inside that chamber, holding on firmly to his love despite all the pain she had caused him.

'Renzo.'

'I am listening to you.'

'What will happen if—if we make a baby?'

'All the usual things, I expect.' He ran his hand seductively up and down her spine. 'Does the idea frighten you?'

'I—I don't know.'

'I suppose it's something we should have talked about.' He spoke thoughtfully. 'A bit selfish of me not to have discussed it with you before we—Jorja, are you trembling?'

'Yes—I don't know why.' But she did know . . . she was on the outside of his heart but she was the one whose body he was enjoying without any of the love he felt for her sister . . . selfish, disloyal, but still the golden girl . . . the one he really made love to!

'I have some Rémy Martin.' Renzo swung himself out of bed. 'You need a brandy.'

He fetched the bottle and a glass, and seated on the side of the four-poster he made Jorja sip the drink until she started to feel warm again . . . warm in body if not in heart.

She gazed at Renzo in the ruby lamplight, made afraid by her own emotions. He reached out a hand and stroked a wing of her hair. 'You said it yourself, *donna*. Too much has happened to you in too short a time and I should have been more aware of this. From a quiet life in the country I make you part of my life and it's natural that you should feel disturbed. Drink a little more brandy.'

She did as he asked, for what he said made sense. Her life at Duncton had never held the excitements which she had been through today. She had never even had a boy-friend so Renzo was the first man in her life, seated there in all his maleness, his eyes upon the velvety smoothness of her shoulders and arms.

Perhaps this was the moment to ask him to set her free so she could go back to the life where she belonged, but the words just wouldn't come. They weren't there any more. The clamorous need for the safety and security of the rectory was replaced by a new set of emotions.

It was no longer possible for her to leave Renzo . . . some essence of him had got right inside her

. . . something more than the physical memory of his possession of her body. What was it Angelica had said to her? That if she fell in love she would lay down body and soul for the man.

It was that . . . knowing it had happened to her the way her sister had predicted which made her shake like an aspen leaf, but thankfully the shakes had gone and with a little sigh she relaxed against the pillows.

'I—I think that's the first nervous attack I ever had. It was very—odd.'

Still with a sombre look in his eyes Renzo took hold of her left hand and held his fingers against her pulse. 'Over excitement.' His smile was faintly quizzical. 'I forget the differences between us, those of age, experience and background.'

But Jorja knew the real truth . . . when he kissed her and his lips grew fierce and wanting, it was Angelica he was kissing. When he touched her and made her senses feel as if they were leaping out of her skin, it was Angelica he was mad to possess.

Jorja felt she could face it. She wasn't about to have the vapours again, just like an authentic village maiden.

'You'll catch cold sitting there.' Her lashes curved down with a touch of shyness. 'Come into bed.'

He finished off the brandy she had left, put away the bottle, then replaced his tawny body alongside hers. His hair was in black disarray against the white pillow, and the lamp diffused an intimate glow around them as they lay side by side.

'I must not forget again how young you are,' he murmured. 'Young and new to the ways of a man.'

Jorja drew her underlip between her teeth, feeling the sensitivity which his kisses had left. 'I don't want to be treated like a—a child.'

'We shall see.' He leaned over her for a breathless moment, then he clicked off the lamp. 'Go to sleep.'

Jorja lay beside him in the darkness, waiting for him to pull her into his arms so they could fall asleep together. But the minutes ticked by and he didn't reach out for her, and Jorja was left with the bleak realisation that the quivering bundle to whom he had given brandy had neither looked nor behaved like the self-possessed golden girl who sauntered along the catwalks of the fashion shows and didn't care a rap whose heart she took and broke.

Tears stung Jorja's eyes. It was a little too late for him to talk about how young and untried she was, as if with a few cool words he could tone down the physical heat which they had shared. He had led her kiss by kiss into the realms of passion, and brought her to responses which had made her cry out almost for his mercy.

It was true that twenty-four hours ago she would have been glad to be left alone, but now she was aching for his arms around her. Like some ruthless potentate in one of those library romances he had imposed himself until not an inch of her could be called her own any more. He had to be aware of what he had done to a total innocent like herself . . . she had never been kissed, but now it was a different story.

There came drifting back into her mind the question she had asked him . . . what would happen if they had made a baby? She lay and thought of the possibility of his darkness and vigour being duplicated into a child which she would carry.

She touched a hand to herself. Here inside her the child of Renzo Talmonte would grow body and limbs and a head of black hair. It would make thrilling movements inside her, letting her know that she wasn't alone, that she was going to be able to hold someone who would belong to her as nothing and nobody ever had. It wouldn't matter, then, if Renzo didn't love her. His child would look at her with loving eyes, and encircle her neck with loving arms. They would be all in all to each other, and she would have given Renzo something he would never receive from Angelica.

Bearing a child meant being pulled out of shape, of being racked by morning sickness, and developing strange fancies for pickles in the middle of the night.

But the end result had to be marvellous, to Jorja's way of thinking, and her way of thinking had never been Angelica's. Her sister was utterly devoted to her own beautiful face and perfect figure; she would never risk them in order to become a mother. She could never love any man enough to let him make her pregnant, but Jorja lay and wondered if Renzo had given her a baby.

She went over in her mind every instant of their day together . . . her senses swam in recollection of his total possession of her, to the very length and breadth of his potent manhood. Oh God, she loved him . . . loved what he had done to her!

Curled on her side of the bed, lapped by the sensuous waves of memory, Jorja fell off to sleep and slept dreamlessly far into the following morning.

She awoke to find herself alone in the bed, and a quick glance around each door revealed that Renzo wasn't in the suite or out on the terrace.

It was another bright morning, and after bathing and putting on a summery white dress with touches of lemon, Jorja decided to go in search of her husband. She wasn't hungry but she longed for a cup of tea and as it was almost eleven o'clock they could possibly share a pot of tea in the lounge downstairs.

Jorja was wandering about in slight mystification, and had decided to take a look in the reading room in the hope that Renzo was there with a newspaper, or was writing a letter at one of the desks, when a voice stopped her in her tracks.

'Hello, sweet face.'

She went to pass the obstruction in flannels and a sea-island shirt, but he caught her by the wrist and she could tell that he wasn't going to let her go without a struggle.

'I missed you in the ballroom last night.'

She gave him a look which might have been

disquieting to someone less complacent. 'I had better things to do,' she retorted.

'All by yourself?' His smile spread into his smallish, pale blue eyes. His fair hair was arranged in a casual cow-lick and showed none of the virile strength of Renzo's hair, being of the type that would probably thin out before he was thirty. Jorja felt a flash of contempt; his looks and his voice jarred on her in a way that Renzo's never did.

'What makes you think I was alone?' she asked. 'I do have a husband.'

'And he was playing cards, sweetie. I saw him go limping in.'

Jorja caught her breath and her eyes flashed up and down the figure in front of her, his porky thighs straining against the grey flannel slacks. 'My husband is more of a man than you'll ever be,' she said furiously. 'He's more fascinating asleep than you are when you're awake!'

The pale blue eyes registered instant shock at the remark, as if never in his spoilt life had someone dared to oppose his self-satisfied opinion of himself. 'You little bitch!' With temper reddening his face he pushed Jorja through the partly open door of the reading room, which was quite unoccupied and had vast windows from ceiling to floor, overlooking a side garden.

Jorja couldn't help feeling dismayed at finding herself alone with this glowering young man, who was pinning her to the wall and pressing his fleshy thighs against her. She could feel their heat through the summery fabric of her dress, and her frantic struggles made him all the more persistent.

'Your airs and graces make me laugh.' His breath fanned her face and muscles stood out in his jaw as he thrust himself against her. 'You're just a cheap little tart who strips and performs in front of a camera, but with that wide-eyed look of yours, sweetie, you could fool an archbishop. It's quite an act you put on.' And holding her hands pinioned he lowered his lips to her left ear. 'Come to my room and show me some of the tricks of your trade.'

His breath was hot, and Jorja could feel him making body movements against her, like some beastly great animal, she thought, as with all her energy she thrust upwards with her knee and hoped she disabled him for the the rest of his stay at Duke's.

As he gaspingly doubled over and nursed his injury, Jorja made a dash from the room, eyes blazing as she crossed the reception area and went out into the sunshine. Her feelings were all churned up. It was unbearable the way Angelica's shadow fell over everything, so that all at once the morning had lost its zest and she couldn't stop thinking of those intimacies which her sister had performed in front of a camera. Intimacies which were supposed to be an expression of love between a woman and a man.

Jorja walked slowly along, hardly aware of the holiday gaiety all around her. The laughter and the talk floated past her ears, and she was blind to the glances which followed her slim figure. It would always be this way, she told herself. Each time she felt a little happiness, there would be some unhappy reminder of the part Angelica played in her life and Renzo's. They would never be free of her, and Jorja lacked the assurance that would have made her sister seem less threatening.

She sat down on one of the seats set among the flower beds along the esplanade. It was no use pretending that Renzo's feelings for her were on a higher plane than those of the wretched young man back at the hotel. Renzo was a distinguished man of the world, but his basic desires were no different . . . not where she was concerned.

It was in this mood of mixed feelings that Jorja noticed the pony. He was one of a trio of ponies who were giving rides to children on the beach, and Jorja felt a lurch of pity at the way the animal hung its head as another child was placed wriggling and energetic on its back. The man in charge gave him a slap and as the pony started to move, it became obvious to Jorja that he was not only lame but overheated and thirsty.

As the child pulled on the bridle and the pony raised its head in weary obedience, Jorja found herself pushing her way through the group of parents to where the owner of the ponies was lighting a cigarette. Maybe it wasn't any of her business, but the utter lack of feeling and comprehension in these people made her heart burn.

'That pony's lame,' she accused the owner. 'If you don't take care he's going to flop down and probably injure the child.'

The man slowly removed his cigarette and stared at her, but not in amazement. Jorja saw from the look in his eyes that he was fully aware of the pony's condition and wasn't in the least concerned that the animal was suffering.

'Why don't you run along, girlie, and mind your own business?' he asked. 'I've been handling ponies for years and I don't need you to tell me my business.'

'I'm quite prepared to report you to the RSPCA,' she retorted. 'If you're going to make your living out of exploiting animals, then you should be made to take proper and humane care of them. That little piebald is not only lame but he's just about ready to keel over—you'll find yourself in real trouble if the child gets hurt and the parents sue for damages.'

This time Jorja had hit a nerve and she knew it. The man dropped his cigarette and stamped his heel on it, then he marched across the beach to where the piebald now stood unmoving except for the weary twitching of its tail. The child was kicking at the pony's sides and urging him to move, but obstinacy had joined forces with pain and the piebald refused to obey its young rider.

'Off with you, sonny.' The child was lifted out of the saddle and returned to the parents, who wanted to know why sonny hadn't had his money's-worth of pony ride.

'The pony's none too bright. Gone a bit lame,' Jorja heard the owner say as she approached the piebald. She stroked his shaggy mane and he gave her a look that made her want to weep.

'You poor little scrap.' She wondered what she could do for him and felt certain she couldn't leave him in the hands of a bully who instead of giving him some care would probably beat him for going lame. Even a visit from the animal welfare people wouldn't guarantee the pony's future treatment, and Jorja had taken a liking to the patient little animal who needed to be rested before he gave any more rides to boisterous children.

'Here goes,' she thought, and zipped open her purse on its shoulder strap. She couldn't imagine what Renzo would say when she turned up with a lame pony, but she hoped he would understand that she never had been able to pass by on the other side of the road when a creature, whether human or animal, had needed a bit of help.

'I'll buy him.' She held out the wad of money to the owner, every pound of it her pocket money from Renzo. 'He deserves a better home than the one he has with you.'

The man glowered down at her. 'You're a right little madam, aren't you? How much you offering? He might be spent out right now, but he's a good worker.'

'I'm giving you fifty pounds,' she said, and she had taken firm hold of the piebald's bridle. 'He won't last much longer with you, and it's more than you'd get from the knacker.'

After a battle of glares, which Jorja was determined to win, the man snatched the money out of her hand. 'All right, he's yours, and you're welcome to him.'

'Has he a name?' she asked, uncaring that people were staring and making comments as the pony exchanged hands.

'I call him Patch.'

'That will do fine,' she said, and led her new acquisition past the gaping onlookers. For the money Renzo was paying for their stay at Duke's they could allow the little fellow into their stable. There would be someone to attend to his lameness and to see that he had a proper meal for a change. He was hers, and to hell with what people thought. She was more than a little weary herself of people and their inhumanities. The majority of them seemed to over-indulge in everything but compassion, and with a look on her face which scorned the looks she and Patch were collecting, she led him along the esplanade at a pace which didn't put too much strain upon his sore leg.

When they appeared in the stable yard at the rear of Duke's four riders were returning from a gallop, and as one of the young women slid from the saddle she let out a laugh. 'Haven't you come to the wrong place?' she asked. 'This hotel doesn't provide stabling for one of those nags from the beach.'

'He's from the beach,' Jorja agreed, 'but he's staying here. I've bought him and I don't think the management will argue with my husband.'

She led Patch to the water trough, where he lowered his weary head and relieved his thirst. After looping his bridle into a wall-ring, Jorja went in search of a stable lad; she wanted oats for the pony and she also required a vet. A lad in a striped jersey was mucking out a stall and she went and spoke to him. 'Him, miss?' He stared towards Patch. 'You kiddin' me?'

'I don't kid about suffering animals,' she said coolly. 'My husband and I are staying here at Duke's, and I want my pony fed and attended to by a vet. You can call the one who deals with the hotel's horses, and don't worry about the bill because I can assure you it will be paid. My name is Signora Talmonte.'

The stable lad gave her a quizzical look and decided not to argue with her. 'Been worked till he's ready for the knacker's yard, miss?' He walked with her to where the pony was lapping the water with a shade more energy, and after talking a look at the lamed leg he gave a whistle of dismay. 'Goin' to cost you a packet in vet's fees.'

'I don't care how much the treatment costs.' Jorja removed the worn old saddle and stirrups and flung them aside. 'I don't know what the people of this country are coming to! There they were, watching with silly smiles while their offspring bumped up and down on this poor fellow's back. It was obvious he was lame.'

'Not everyone's got your kind heart, miss.' The stable lad grinned at her. 'The manager of Duke's is hardly famous for his soft heart and I can't see him letting this pony of yours stay here among the thoroughbreds. No, miss, he won't buy it.'

'He's got to.' Jorja stroked her fingers through the pony's tangled mane. 'Renzo will see to it —he's my husband and he usually gets what he wants from people. Now how about getting me some oats for Patch?'

'If you say so, miss.' The lad was whistling as he crossed the yard, but he broke off as two men appeared, one of them arguing and gesticulating while the other calmly listened as they approached Jorja and the pony. She felt instant relief at seeing Renzo, and guessed that the riders who had seen her enter with Patch had gone to the management and kicked up a fuss about both of them.

'This animal will have to be removed.' The manager shared an affronted look between Jorja and Patch. 'This just will not do, *signora*. We cannot allow such a creature on the premises; it is quite against our rules.'

'Most rules have a certain pliability, or such has been my experience.' Renzo was looking steadily at Jorja as he spoke but she couldn't tell if he was amused or annoyed by her purchase of a poor weary beast who nuzzled her shoulder as if his animal instincts were telling him that she was the only person in the world who cared what became of him.

She fixed her blue eyes upon Renzo's face and put every ounce of appeal into that look. She knew only too well that when he chose to be forceful there were few people who had the nerve to oppose him, and she wanted him to defend her action in bringing the pony to a stable where he could be taken care of.

Renzo reached out a hand and ran it along the pony's back, feeling the thrust of the ribs beneath the piebald hide. Then he swung to face the hotel manager, and Jorja knew it was no accident that he slightly raised his ebony stick. 'You would charge well to stable a thoroughbred,' he said, 'so charge me the same rate for the pony.'

'But the animal could be infectious.' The manager was looking down his nose at Patch, who waited in a patient kind of daze for kicks or kindness. Jorja patted him to let him know that he could rely on her for the kindness.

'He's lame and underfed,' Renzo said decisively. 'I think you will take him in, *signore*. It would be humane, as well as good business, eh?'

'This really is against my principles——' The manager continued to look doubtful.

'What are principles when an act of kindness is at stake?' Once again Renzo's eyes flicked Jorja's face in a look which she couldn't quite read. 'With some care the animal will begin to look quite respectable in a few days, and I would hate you to disappoint my wife, *signore*, by refusing to stable the pony. She's set on it, as you can see.'

The manager gave Jorja a rather helpless look, for standing there in her white dress, her arm about the neck of her pony, her eyes so intensely blue, she had something about her that reflected both challenge and vulnerability.

Abruptly he relented. 'I ask only one thing of you, *signora*,' his smile came and went, 'don't make a crusade of bringing to my hotel any more animals in distress. It isn't that I am unsympathetic, but not all my guests have your benevolent nature.'

'Thank you,' she murmured. 'I am grateful.'

'Then the matter is settled?' Renzo asked. 'If there are further complaints, you will let it be known that the stabling of the pony has your approval, *signore*?'

'Complaints come with the responsibility of running an hotel,' the manager said, resignedly. 'I will leave you to deal with the stable hands, Signore Talmonte. You seem more than capable of getting people to do your bidding.'

The moment they were left on their own, Jorja gave Renzo a smile which he didn't return. He stood looking down at her, slightly shaking his head as if he found her something of an imponderable. 'I can't leave you alone for half an hour, can I?' he murmured. 'I had business at the bank, and in that short time you manage to become the owner of a bag of bones who couldn't win a three-legged race. How did it happen, eh?'

She regaled him with the details, and now that the manager had made his departure the lad in the striped shirt appeared with half a bag of oats and latched them around the pony's neck. 'Got your own way, did you, miss?' he grinned.

'With the help of my husband.' Jorja watched with satisfaction as Patch tucked into the oats. 'We have to speak with the man in charge of the stables—is he around?'

The lad glanced up at the stable clock, which was attached to the stone archway which led into the yard. 'He pops out for a Guinness around this time, miss, but he'll be back in about half an hour. Old Duffy's all right. Likes anything on four legs, and he can't abide some of the snobs who come to Duke's. Says they're not the real upper crust any more, apart from one or two.'

The cheeky green eyes flickered towards Renzo, as if taking note that he was the genuine article as he stood there in a perfectly cut, light beige suit that intensified his air of Italian *arroganza*.

'What's your name?' Renzo asked him.

'Freddy, sir.'

'Then I shall trust you, Freddy, to take care of the pony and arrange for the vet to see him as soon as possible.'

'Glad to oblige, sir.' Freddy tucked his tip into a pocket of his grubby breeches. 'It must have been Patch's lucky day, getting himself noticed by your missus.'

'Yes,' Renzo drawled, 'my missus must have had her heart on fire with good resolution this morning. Bid *arrivederci* to your somewhat bedraggled pet, my dear. It will soon be time for lunch.'

'See you soon, Patch.' Jorja felt warmly pleased with her morning's work, and this was in the smile she gave Freddy. 'I'll be along this afternoon to see him and to hear what the vet had to say about his leg. Don't forget to tell Mr Duffy that it's all above-board for Patch to be stabled here.'

'It's going to put a few noses out of joint,' Freddy said gleefully. 'Patch is looking brighter, miss, now he's got some oats in his belly.'

'Yes, poor old love.'

'He isn't the only one who needs his oats,' Renzo remarked, taking Jorja firmly by the elbow. 'Are you going to join me for lunch, young woman, or do you prefer to stay here?'

'I'm coming, *signore*.' As she walked with Renzo to the side entrance of the hotel she glanced up at him. 'I couldn't help myself—you aren't annoyed, are you?'

'No.'

'Then what are you thinking?'

'That I am anxious to be alone with you.'

'Oh dear——'

'No need for alarm.' He laughed briefly. 'I want to kiss you.'

As they rode up in the lift there was a tension between them which found its relief the moment he closed the door of their suite and tossed his stick to a chair. He caught Jorja's slim body into his arms and pressed her to him. His eyes were brilliantly alive as they held her gaze . . . held it until her lashes fluttered and her hands pressed against the nape of his neck.

'I don't even start to know you,' he murmured against her mouth. 'You keep surprising me.'

'I often surprise myself.' Their lips met with a sensuousness that turned to hunger, and whatever her resolve of the night before it was abandoned as she sank with him to the couch and lay in his arms, enjoying his kisses and the feel of his hands on her body.

'You did mention lunch.' Her eyes played with his.

'I mentioned oats.'

Laughing, she ran ahead of him into the bedroom, peeling off her dress, kicking off her shoes, laughter fading to a catch of desire as he stood over her and flung off his jacket. Her hands reached up and assisted with his tie, and in another half-minute he was gathering her willing body close to his.

They came together without preliminary, the sunlight through the windows bathing them in its warm beneficence. Their passion was generous and exultant, white limbs locked with hard brown ones, slim hands moving up and down the supple muscles from shoulder to thigh. The vibrant throbs, the deep and quickening thrills drove Jorja to incoherence . . . to a wanton wildness of feeling.

'Darling, darling.' She clutched him with pleasured desperation.

Strong hands supporting the small of her back, Renzo raised her to him until their pulses fused into one resounding beat, held and shared until the tremolo quivered into a stillness of bronze flesh welded to white and softest gold.

'Oh—girl!' His breath raked across her throat and she felt the hammering of his heart against her breast, a motion which actually stirred her sensitive skin.

They lay there with their bodies unified, and Jorja's lips trembled into a smile as she felt the excitation of her innermost nerves. How could anything on earth be more wondrous than the unity she had just experienced with Renzo? She would like to stay like this for ever and never have to see or speak to anyone but him. She wanted nobody else in all the world. He sufficed. He was the centre of her being and her one and only necessity.

She threaded her fingers through his thick black hair and thought briefly of the lascivious young man who had pressed her up against the wall of the reading room. He had made physical desire seem cheap and nasty, and she quickly pushed him out of her mind and tenderly kissed Renzo's mouth with softly parted lips. Love trembled inside her but before she could speak the telephone started to ring, filling the room with the intrusive clamour of the world they had forgotten for a while.

The telephone was at the bedside and with a slight groan, but without disengaging himself from Jorja, Renzo reached for the instrument.

He seemed to listen for a long time, and Jorja couldn't help but realise that whoever was on the line had imparted some information which had effectively cooled Renzo's ardour.

'Drat the thing,' Jorja muttered, and she meant the telephone. As she lay wondering who could be speaking to him at such length, a sudden shiver ran over her bare body and she drew the sheet around her. Why didn't he break in and say he was on his honeymoon and not to be disturbed? Jorja ran her hand up and down his muscular arm, feeling the tickle of the dark hair against her palm and realising from the face of the bedside clock that they had spent their lunchtime satisfying a hunger of the senses rather than the stomach. She tried to recapture those tempestuous, shameless longings which had been so piercingly pleasured. She was lapped by a more mellow pleasure as her eyes measured the tawny shoulders of the man who could make her abandon all restraint when he took her to bed. The muscles beneath his skin were defined in a Rodin way as he inclined towards the telephone, and then she heard him say:

'*Si*, you were right to call me, Flavia. I will indeed pass on to Jorja your sincere regrets. *Arrivederci*.'

The ting of the replaced receiver touched Jorja upon a nerve.

'What is it, Renzo?' Her fingers clutched his arm, feeling the tension in the muscles.

'Our honeymoon is over.' He spoke with finality. 'I must return to London.'

'Over——?' Jorja scanned his face and felt as if her heart was beating out a warning.

'I regret so.' And he explained that a telex had arrived at his office from his sister-in-law, bearing the information that his mother was flying to London to consult a Harley Street specialist. It seemed that her plans had been made all of a sudden, and Monica was anxious that Renzo should be at the airport to meet her. The specialist she would be seeing was a heart man.

'Of course we must return.' Jorja was instantly concerned for his mother, but it took an effort to conceal her desperate sense of disappointment. She had begun to hope that their stay at Sandbourne would bind them together, so that no one could come between them, but it wasn't to be. Already he was reaching for his robe and wearing a look which excluded her from his thoughts, his brows drawn into a dark concealing arch as he tied the belt.

'*Madre* suffered a stroke about two years ago,' he said, 'and ever since she has been on medication. It now seems that she is having bad palpitations and the medicine has become ineffective.'

He stood there in thought, then raised his gaze to Jorja. 'We must arrange for our belongings to be packed—unless you would like to stay on at Duke's for the rest of the fortnight?'

'Oh no,' she said at once. 'I want to come with you.'

'Do you?' He stood regarding her as she knelt on the honeymoon bed with the sheet sliding down her body. 'What of your precious pony?'

'They'll provide a horse-box when he's fit to travel.' She spoke with certainty because she could see that Renzo was abstracted by his thoughts. They were centred on his mother, the woman he hadn't even mentioned . . . as if it had always been his plan to keep Jorja apart from the important aspects of his life. Deep inside she was hurt, because there inside he had made her so vulnerable, so that what mattered to him was her concern as well.

'Darling,' she spoke softly, 'we should eat before we leave.'

He nodded, then just as quickly shook his

head. 'No, we can stop on the way home. The sooner we get started the better.'

'All right,' she agreed, and though the sun was still shining into the room, Jorja no longer felt a golden glow at the very centre of her being.

A shadow had come between Renzo and herself, for now he was looking at her with a frown. 'Do get dressed,' he said, and as he turned away from her, he was lighting a cigar, the smoke drifting back at her as he walked into the sitting-room and left her alone.

For several minutes Jorja gnawed her lip in indecision, for there seemed so much to do all of a sudden. Then she climbed out of bed, dressed quickly in pants and a shirt, and telephoned room-service for a maid to come and do their packing. She next asked for reception and told the young woman to make up their bill as they had been called back urgently to London.

The remainder of Jorja's honeymoon at Duke's was spent down in the stable where the vet had seen to Patch but was still in attendance upon one of the horses. He assured her that Patch would be bright as brass in a few days. He was a tough little beggar and with some grooming and feeding up he should make a champion pet for a child, if she had one as yet.

'No.' She smiled and shook her head . . . but inwardly wondered if some fluke of fate meant Patch, the abused pony from the beach at Sandbourne, to fulfil the role of pet to a child she might bear Renzo. In view of the ardour he had lavished upon her there was a good chance of it happening, but as she made arrangements for Patch to be delivered to Hanson Square as soon as he was fit for the journey, Jorja felt sorry to be leaving this big white hotel facing the sea.

Her honeymoon might have been cut short, but every moment of it had been memorable. She had arrived here an apprehensive girl, and was leaving with a whole new slant on what it meant to be a woman.

CHAPTER SEVEN

RENZO didn't suggest that Jorja go with him to Heathrow Airport to meet his mother. His manner at breakfast was withdrawn and she saw a look of worry carved into his face as he drank his coffee.

'*Madre* is very fond of white flowers.' He spoke abruptly. 'Be so good as to order a large selection from Gudrun's and have them placed in her bedroom and sitting-room. Also make sure that she has a television set and a radio. It's been some time since the Contessa stayed here, and I only wish that her visit wasn't occasioned by her state of health.'

Jorja ate another spoonful of grapefruit and felt the sharpness against the edge of her teeth. This morning she felt desperately young and left out of his innermost thoughts. She wore a filmy silk nightdress and wrap, but inwardly she had somehow reverted to the girl whose life had revolved around her father's rectory. Something in Renzo's manner had nipped like frost her budding confidence.

'I know so little about your mother,' she said, and back into her voice had crept a touch of apprehension.

'Do men discuss their mothers on their honeymoon?' he asked.

'N-no, I suppose not.' She spoke diffidently. 'But you're so—well, you don't talk to me about your family and I—I need to know a little more than I do. For instance——'

He raised an eyebrow, seated across from the silver coffee set and the fine china with the golden rims, here in this gracious breakfast-room on the second floor of his Georgian house. 'For instance?'

'Is your mother a real *contessa*?' Jorja flushed as she spoke; she didn't want him to think her a snob but it was rather exciting, the thought of having a titled mother-in-law.

'I sincerely believe so,' he drawled.

'Renzo,' Jorja felt deflated by his attitude, 'you're treating me as if I haven't any right to mention her. I suppose you are going to introduce the two of us?'

He frowned and his gaze seemed transfixed by the sunlit glitter of the coffee pot. 'You might as well know that she has no idea I am married. She probably imagines that I am still engaged to your sister. We decided, Stelvio's wife and I, that *madre* shouldn't be told that he had left home in order to live with Angelica. The condition of her heart had to be borne in mind, and both Monica and I felt that Stelvio's infatuation would be short-lived.'

Jorja absorbed his words, then felt their impact with a sense of shock. 'I see, Renzo! No wonder you asked me if I'd like to stay on at Sandbourne —I would have been out of sight and out of mind!'

'For the time being it would have made things easier,' he agreed. 'Eventually I could have explained the true state of affairs.'

'And now you have to explain why you're married to me instead of Angelica?' Jorja's eyes held fiery blue lights as she gazed across at him. 'What a tangle it all is! Naturally your mother will want to know why your engagement was broken.'

'Of a certainty.' He returned Jorja's look broodingly.

'And you certainly can't tell her the truth; it would be too much of a shock.'

'I quite agree,' he said emphatically. 'Stelvio is her golden boy and she would accept his infidelity with great pain.'

'Then what are you going to tell her, Renzo?'

'That Angelica decided on a career in preference to being a wife, so I married you instead.'

'Sounds reasonable,' Jorja agreed, though she was thinking secretly that it placed her in the category where she seemed to belong . . . the second-best choice.

'You haven't eaten much breakfast,' she murmured.

'I'm not particularly hungry.'

'You mustn't be too anxious.' Jorja pleated her linen napkin. 'So you are the Conte Talmonte?'

'I don't use the title. I dispensed with it because I wanted to make my way in the world and the idea persists that the aristocracy are but players of the game rather than hard-headed men and women of business or talent.'

'Did Angelica know about your title?' Asking the question was difficult but Jorja was curious about this aspect of his relationship with her sister.

'She discovered its existence when she met Stelvio. She was, of course, interested in the idea of becoming a *contessa* but by then I had realised that she was two-timing me.' His lips thinned as he spoke and his eyes were the hard grey that made Jorja feel cold. 'You are my titled lady, are you not, even if I choose to keep the title under the rose.'

'Under—the rose?' Jorja looked intrigued.

'Long ago in rooms of secret meetings the ceiling had a rose medallion under which the vow of secrecy was made.' For the first time that morning he smiled, and rising to his feet he came around the table to Jorja, brushed the hair from her brow and pressed his lips there.

'Is that in place of a tiara?' she murmured, and she admired the look of him in a finely striped brown suit with a wide striped beige shirt. A quiver ran from the nape of her neck to the very base of her spine, for she had grown so sensitive to his touch that the slightest advance from him could fire her with longing. It was, in a way, as frightening as it was exciting to be so aware of a man. He could make her feel a shameless longing with a look. He could make her shameless with just a stroke of his hand, which was happening now as he drew his fingers through her hair and allowed them to wander down the side of her neck to her shoulder in the filmy fabric of her wrap.

'I have to be going now, *donna*, if I'm to be on time for *madre*'s flight.' He drew her to her feet as he spoke and held her pressed to him. 'I shall explain matters in a satisfactory way to my mother so don't spend the next few hours in trepidation. Remember the flowers and discuss luncheon with Mrs Alberti the cook. Be firm but engaging with the staff; they expect it of the mistress of the house.'

'It's a very fine house, Renzo.'

'It is rather special.' As he spoke he studied her upraised face, framing it with his hands as he slowly kissed her mouth. 'You taste of marmalade, *cara mia*, and despite the fancy nightwear you look rather like a prim little girl who doesn't quite know where she belongs. Is that the way you feel?'

'A little,' she confessed. 'I want your mother to like me—do you think she will?'

'I like you, don't I?' he said casually. He let go of her and shot a look at his wristwatch. 'I must fly! Make yourself at home, Jorja, and do rest assured that the Contessa will find you as charming as I do—in a manner of speaking.' A brief smile flicked his lips as he left Jorja standing in a ray of sunlight through the long Georgian windows. *'Arrivederci!'*

'See you soon,' she murmured, and couldn't help the slight wave of despondency which swept over her as the door closed behind him. Now she was all on her own in a strange house in

a city she hardly knew, and she couldn't relax in
the assurance that Renzo loved her. Only moments ago he had used a nice enough word, but
to be liked by him wasn't the same as being madly
adored by him.

'May I clear the table, madam?' The maid Sylvia
had entered the breakfast-room, and bearing
Renzo's instructions in mind Jorja strove to look
composed, as if she had been dealing with
maids and a butler, not to mention a cook, all
her life.

'Yes, I am quite finished, and when I've
showered and dressed I'd like to take a look at the
Contessa's suite to make sure everything is nice.
I'm ordering flowers for her rooms, and my husband is anxious that she should have a television
set and a radio.'

'I'm sure you'll find everything in order,
madam.' Sylvia spoke in a slightly distant manner. 'Miss Scott was here yesterday and she gave
orders to Torrence that the Contessa was to be
made as comfortable as possible.'

'Good.' Jorja tried not to feel that her presence
at Hanson Square was irrelevant. Flavia Scott had
proved that she was indispensable to Renzo, but
Jorja had doubts about her own place in his life.
Especially since he had told her that his mother
knew nothing about his marriage, as if it were
something that he didn't take seriously . . .
something that he still looked upon as a means of
retaliation; a weapon to be used in his emotional
war against Angelica.

Jorja chided herself for supposing that his

sensual enjoyment of her was any indication
that she was important to him outside the
bedroom.

And their bedroom at Hanson Square was a
beautiful room set in a curving Georgian bay that
made time stand still when Jorja walked in
through the rosewood doors with their antique
fittings. Every item of furniture had been chosen
by someone with an intrinsic eye for real beauty
and Jorja didn't need anyone to tell her that
Renzo had spent considerable time and money
on making his London house as superb on the
inside as it was mellow and gracious on the
outside.

She walked through to the bathroom, which in
days gone by would have been the room where
the master kept his powdered wigs and robes of
office, for Renzo had told her that in Georgian
times this house had been the home of a renowned hanging judge, feared and admired for
the way he dealt with criminals. A painting of
him in his scarlet robes still hung in the hall, a
further sign, had Jorja needed one, that Renzo
believed in stern justice for offenders.

The bathroom was panelled in ivory tiles, with
a deep, sable-coloured tub into which the water
gushed from a special fitting which swirled it into
a mass of scented bubbles, like a great Roman
goblet of champagne, Jorja thought, as she slid
into the tub. Why bother with a quick shower
when Flavia Scott had already been to the house
to ensure that everything was made ready for
Renzo's mother? She had all the morning ahead

of her, her only task the ordering of the white flowers.

In fact there was a telephone connection in the bathroom, and feeling like one of those luxurious creatures in a Hollywood film, Jorja dialled the operator and asked for the number of Gudrun's flower shop in the Strand.

She dallied over the order, listening to descriptions of various white blooms, from huge Chinese chrysanthemums to tiny lilies of the valley. She finally decided on mixed sprays in straw baskets and requested that they be delivered by noon, adding with a touch of pride:

'The flowers are for my mother-in-law, the Contessa Talmonte, who is arriving from Italy to stay with my husband and myself.'

She was immediately assured that the sprays would be delivered on time and Gudrun's felt confident that madam would find the flowers beautiful and fresh.

Jorja lay watching the rise and fall of her slim legs in the bubbly water, a buoyant sensation which mingled with the fragrant aroma of bath essence to make her feel like a houri in a sultan's palace, satin-smooth and glowing for his delectation. Rather naughty thoughts for a rector's daughter, she thought with a smile. Yet the only kind of thoughts it was wise to have in relation to Renzo.

As the water swirled around her hips she wondered what kind of a woman his mother was. Was she haughty and superbly dressed by a

Roman couturier? Was she possessive of her handsome sons and likely to resent a daughter-in-law whom she had never met?

Tingling all over Jorja climbed out of the sable tub, and as she reached for a huge terrycloth towel and wrapped it around her, she knew from what Renzo had left unsaid that morning that his mother had met and approved of Angelica. Jorja knew that her sister had charmed his mother, smiling that dazzling smile of hers and showing not a sign of the selfishness which lay at the heart of her like a peachstone in the centre of one of the most luscious of fruits.

Jorja slowly applied perfumed body velvet, working the lovely Nocturnes scent into her skin. She couldn't dazzle Renzo's mother, or convince her that she was the one and only woman for him, but she could smell nice and look sincere. She couldn't pretend to have the glamour which blinded most people to Angelica's wilful love of herself, and she had already decided to wear a blue cotton-cambric dress with neat pin-tucking on the bodice. She wanted no pretence between herself and the Contessa. They would meet and they would either like or dislike each other. There were no guarantees and Jorja was expecting none, for it seemed as if she walked on a silken tightrope, taking one step at a time.

After she had dried her hair and looped it casually at the nape of her neck, she put on her blue dress and eyed herself in the Regency pier-glass which stood by the window so that she had a very clear image of herself. Did she look like a wife? Was it believable that she was the mistress of this tall Georgian house in the heart of London?

Perhaps she would feel more like the mistress after she had taken a look at the various rooms and acquainted herself with the plan of the house.

She made her way down to the hall where the sunlight through the long, many-paned windows made a checkerboard across the mellow wooden floor. Jorja rested a moment against the balustrade of the stairs, for her gaze had been caught by the portrait of the hanging judge, his eyes dark and pitiless beneath the silvery wig. She didn't think she liked him and felt as if his eyes followed her across the hall and in through the doorway of a splendid room, with bay windows in deep embrasures, and a cool green Adam ceiling with gold-flecked cornices. At the centre of the ceiling hung a chandelier which had to be Venetian, so fabulous was its design. It was like an immense jewel which would glow and sparkle when it was alight.

Jorja admired the elegant sofas upholstered in figured silk, rose-coloured with hints of pale green. And most of all above the rose-marble fireplace she liked a lovely painting of a little girl with ringlets seated on a big silk cushion. Going closer she studied the signature in the corner and saw that the child had been painted by George Romney.

A discreet cough attracted her attention and when she turned round, Torrence the butler was

standing in the doorway giving her a slightly
old-fashioned look. 'Would you like coffee and
biscuits served in the garden room, madam?' he
asked, and as he spoke the Dresden clock on the
mantelpiece began to chime and she saw that it
was eleven o'clock.

'This is the drawing-room, isn't it, Torrence?'

'It is indeed, madam.'

'It's quite splendid—do those doors lead into
the dining-room?'

'They do, madam.'

Jorja was aware that Torrence wasn't in the
least fooled by her. He knew that she came from a
shabby genteel background and had never lived
in a house like this before. Its mellow richness
was far removed from the stone-walled rectory at
Duncton, where much of the furniture had been
used by a succession of rectors.

'I would like a cup of coffee in the garden
room,' she said. 'If you'll show me the way.'

'By all means, madam.'

Jorja followed him to where a pair of floral
ironwork gates led into an hexagonal-shaped
room which appeared to be part of the garden
because it was completely glazed, overlooking
the lawn and the trees from every angle. There
was a suite of bamboo furniture, including a
chaise-longue cushioned in leaf-green and
oyster-white, great tubs of geraniums, and a
pagan figure of Pan piping water into a stone
pool.

It was a delightful, rather unexpected place,
where Jorja felt more at home than in the beauti-

ful indoor rooms of the house. She turned with a smile to Torrence, who gave her a rather solemn look in return. 'Are there fish in the pool?' she asked.

'Beneath the lily pads, madam. An assortment of them in gold, silver and black. When they are fed around noon they soon make an appearance; their food is kept in that container.'

He indicated what looked like a valuable Chinese vase with a dragon lid. 'I will have your coffee brought to you, madam.' And with a slight bow Torrence left Jorja to explore the delights of the garden room.

There was even a bamboo bookcase with an assortment of volumes on its shelves, and a cassette player on a cabinet filled with cassettes, and Jorja had visions of Renzo sitting here in the dusk, smoking a cigar and listening to music as the scents of the garden stole in through the windows.

A little later she sat on one of the deep sills drinking her coffee and watching a song thrush with a speckled breast go hopping across the velvety green lawn. There were banks of ornamental shrubs along with trees that Jorja as a country girl instantly recognised. A magnificent beech tree whose branches swept the ground, a pair of weeping birches, some lovely willow oaks, and cherry and plum trees that in the springtime would be laden with blossom.

How strange that this was a town garden when everything looked so peaceful. The chirping birds were undisturbed and for a little while Jorja could pretend that time had stood still, and that nothing beyond this garden could disturb the tranquillity which she felt right now.

She could almost forget that by now Renzo had greeted his mother at the airport and was at this precise moment driving her to Hanson Square. For a while she felt secure, for all her life she had loved the things that were nature's. They weren't only lovely, they were unpretentious and un-affected by the horde of emotions which could assail human beings. They followed age-old laws and clung to habits which were never despoiled by the march of so-called progress created by men and women.

Long ago in this garden, whose high, mellow brick walls shielded its privacy, women in crino-line skirts had wandered among the beds of flowers, or played croquet on the lawn. Whether true or false it had seemed an age of quality rather than quantity. The architecture had been superb, the paintings had been full of living detail, and craftsmen had fashioned lovely things in wood and silver.

Jorja didn't doubt that Renzo felt akin to days past rather than these modern times. The very look of him, and the way he behaved with a woman, indicated a man who would have been ideally suited to a Georgian way of life.

Jorja watched the sunlight flicker and burn in her wedding ring. It would have been better for their marriage had they been able to adjust to each other without the strain of pretending to the

Contessa that Angelica was out of his life for good. But his brother was the man involved with Angelica and it would be traumatic if the truth came out.

From an infant Jorja had known all about the ten commandments. To her way of thinking there was a certain grandeur about them, these laws written by Moses upon tablets of stone. It seemed to her that the truth was so much stronger than deception that in the end it blasted its way out of a tunnel of lies and let in the white-hot, searing light in which the deceivers twisted and turned like trapped moths.

Though she felt the sun on her skin, Jorja felt a shiver of apprehension. The garden looked so serene, while inside the house a warm welcome was being arranged for Renzo's mother. Her own anxiety would be at a normal level, if only her marriage was normal, so that when the Contessa arrived she could greet her in the happy knowledge that she was at the heart of Renzo like his blood beat; that no one, no circumstances on earth could disrupt their lives.

Instead she had to pretend that nothing could glide like a serpent into their Eden. She had to look as if Renzo worshipped the ground she walked on. He would expect it of her in front of his mother, for it would combat her natural curiosity as to why he had switched his affections from one sister to the other.

Jorja glanced at her watch and saw that it was a few minutes after noon. Aware of the tension in her body she went across to the fish pool and took tiny pellets of food from the Chinese vase; the moment she started to drop in the food the fish appeared from beneath the heart-shaped lily leaves, waggling their graceful tails as they went for the pellets, a mill of glistening bodies which Jorja watched with fascination.

She was sitting there on the stone rim of the pool when a maid came to inform her that the flowers from Gudrun's had just arrived.

'Good.' Jorja rose to her feet. 'I'll come and arrange them for the Contessa.'

The hall was full of their scent, and for the next half-hour Jorja was occupied in the Contessa's suite of rooms. The walls of the bedroom and sitting-room were hung with Chinese silk paper, and most of the furniture was Chippendale. Never in her life had Jorja seen a more elegant bed, with its damask canopy and its mound of satin baby pillows. The deep soft rug almost covered the floor, and the drapes at the windows were also of rose damask.

Jorja nodded to herself, satisfied that the baskets of white flowers looked and smelled heavenly. In the sitting-room an ivory-coloured television set had been installed, and on a bow-legged little table beside the daybed there was a radio and a bowl of fruit.

A haven had been provided for Renzo's mother, and Jorja prayed that nothing would happen during her visit to cause her to be upset. Her health was obviously on the decline, and Renzo had spoken of his brother as being their mother's golden boy, so often the case with a younger son, as if a mother felt that all the father's strength of character or personality had gone into the first born, her second child being more akin to herself.

Jorja returned to the bedroom for a final inspection, and once again she admired the perfection of it. A bedroom of charm, comfort and escapism, with embroidered sheets and pillowcases on the bed, a Queen Anne chair with a matching footrest, and lamps with Derby figurines as their base, the tiny bare feet amid leaves and crushed pink roses.

A memory of her own mother stole into Jorja's mind, and the way she had died quietly and bravely in the shabby front bedroom of the rectory. It had been the saddest day of Jorja's life, and she very much hoped that Renzo's mother would respond to the treatment she hoped to find in London. The Talmontes could afford the very best of doctors, but it wasn't always the case that money could stave off the hand of death. It reached out for rich and poor alike, but at least the Contessa would have every comfort, and the firm shoulder of her eldest son to lean upon.

As Jorja closed the door on the fragrance of the many white flowers, she had a mental vision of Renzo's shoulders and the way the muscles moved beneath his skin. Oh yes, he was so good to lean on, his warm skin blending with hers, his arrant maleness seducing the very breath out of her. She felt sure his mother would soon realise that she was totally infatuated with the look and touch of him.

And with this thought in mind Jorja was smiling to herself as she made her way down the graceful curve of the staircase, trailing her fingers along the mahogany handrail. She had almost reached the foot of the stairs when there was a sound of car wheels on the driveway. Jorja hesitated, then impulsively she crossed the hall to the front door and opened it.

Yes, it was the Rolls, and Renzo was opening the passenger door and extending a helping hand to the Contessa. The woman who emerged from the big car was surprisingly petite, especially so beside the tall figure of her son.

As they turned towards the house they saw Jorja standing on the steps in the sunlight. The Contessa caught Renzo by the arm and said something in Italian. Though Jorja didn't understand the language she right away guessed the content of the remark. Renzo's mother had seen her resemblance to Angelica and commented on it, and in so doing had hardened his eyes as they swept Jorja from head to heel.

She felt a shrinking inside her. Would the reaction to her always be the same, making her the mirror in which her sister seemed to be reflected? At Duncton it had rarely happened. Everyone there had grown used to seeing Jorja in her role of housekeeper.

It was in these more exotic surroundings that she reflected facets of Angelica which were to do with costly clothes, and a sheen on her hair and skin which had a lot to do with Renzo. As he and his mother approached the house, Jorja tried to forget that she was as nervous as a cat, just as she had been on her wedding day, a stranger among strangers with no one of her own to support her. She stood straight and slim and shaped her mouth into a smile, reflecting that the best way to fight her nervousness was to let her being flood with her feelings for Renzo.

After all, Angelica was miles away from Hanson Square, and she was the girl who had lain in Renzo's arms last night and known every inch of his body even if his heart remained a mystery to her.

The Contessa Evalina Talmonte was supported by Renzo's arm as she came slowly up the steps to the portico, exquisitely dressed in a pale beige suite and close-fitting hat; a woman who possessed a timeless elegance and breeding. Her luminous dark eyes, shaded beneath by tiny shadows, dwelt on Jorja's face as Renzo introduced them to each other. Her complexion was still very lovely but it was obvious that her journey had tired her.

'So,' she murmured, 'you are the surprise which Renzo had in store for me?'

'Yes, *contessa*.' Jorja's smile was much less strained, for there was nothing intimidating about her mother-in-law. The relief was immense, for Jorja felt quite certain that she could care for this gracious woman with the beautiful Italian eyes about whom there clung a fragility which had to be intensely worrying for Renzo. It was also a relief that she hadn't travelled to England alone, for a middle-aged woman had emerged from the Rolls, clasping in her hand a leather vanity-case and carrying over her arm a creamy mink wrap.

They entered the house and the Contessa gave a sigh, as of someone deeply glad to have reached her destination. She reached out and took hold of Jorja's left hand, her gaze upon the wedding ring which still looked so very new. 'It all happened quite suddenly, eh? That would seem to be the way of things these days, and I wonder if you young people take seriously any more the attachments and vows that people of my generation thought of as—holy.'

The luminous dark eyes met Jorja's blue ones, searching them with the expected curiosity of a woman only recently informed of her son's broken engagement to Angelica. 'We meet now, and it will be nice, Jorja, the getting to know each other.'

'Oh yes,' Jorja said fervently. 'I lost my own mother a long time ago and it will be lovely, being friends with Renzo's mother.'

The Contessa smiled and glanced at her son, who was regarding the two of them with a certain gravity. 'You said she was young, *caro*, but you forgot to mention that she is charming.'

'I suppose she is,' he mocked. 'Now, *madonnina*, I want you to go straight to your own apartment for a short rest before we sit down to lunch.'

'I would like that,' his mother agreed, and then before she could stop him, Renzo had lifted her slight figure into his arms and, as he made his way upstairs with her, Jorja watched anxiously, half-afraid he would stumble even though he took his time because of his leg. She followed with the Contessa's companion, and they in turn were followed by a manservant with several items of luggage.

'The Contessa should not have risked this journey to England.' The companion spoke in an anxious tone of voice to Jorja, her accent and manner those of an educated woman. 'She knows there are doctors of equal quality in Rome but her main wish was to see her son, you comprehend, *signora*?'

Jorja met the woman's eyes and saw shades of fear in them. 'Has the Contessa been—very unwell?' Jorja spoke in a low tone of voice as they proceeded along the panelled gallery to where her mother-in-law's suite was situated.

'She has been far from well, *signora*, and on the aircraft she had a bad spell of palpitations. The Contessa is not a woman to complain, and she endures the fact that her sons live many miles from Florence. She has always wanted them to succeed in life and is so proud that both have made their mark.'

Jorja nodded, but her heart sank at the way Stelvio Talmonte had strayed into an affaire with Angelica. No wonder Renzo was so concerned that the facts of the relationship be kept from his mother; none of them had to be medical people in order to see that the Contessa was ailing.

Despite her fatigue she was delighted with her

rooms and their air of comfort and welcome. *'Cara,'* she again clasped Jorja's hand, 'I love white flowers because their scent is so vivid. My Renzo must have told you how much I like them.'

'Yes, he did mention that you were fond of them.' Jorja gave him a questing look, hoping he approved of the graceful lilies, huge daisies, and tall ivory gladioli which brightened his mother's eyes. He stood tall between the Georgian windows and she saw the edge of his handsome mouth dent into a smile.

'I believe my young wife has been nervous, *madre*, in case you found her not to your liking. She is unusually modest for a young woman of these days, but certainly not a mouse.'

The Contessa gave him a considering look as she removed her hat and revealed dark hair traced with silver. 'When you decided to be a cosmopolitan, *caro*, I thought it unlikely that you would marry a girl of simplicity. It seemed that you had set your mind on—' His mother paused, and for Jorja it was a significant pause. 'But people change their minds more rapidly these days, which is but a sign of the restless times in which we live. Ah, but it is so peaceful here, such an oasis after the bustle of the airport and the streams of traffic.'

She sank into the Queen Anne chair and beckoned Jorja to the footrest. 'I live very quietly with my good friend and companion, Cosima,' she indicated the woman who had begun to unpack the suitcases, 'in a villa on the outskirts of

Florence. You must visit us, *cara*, when I have seen my specialist and he gives me treatment which, I hope, will subdue my throbs as I call them.'

'*Madre*, do you suffer any pain?' Renzo looked at her with serious eyes. 'Come, tell me!'

She leaned back in the cushioned chair, and Jorja studied her lovely Latin bone-structure overlaid by soft olive skin. She could almost feel the worry and concern which had a grip on Renzo.

'No pain,' his mother assured him, 'but I tire too quickly, and Cosima has to bank up my pillows because of the palpitations which affect me when I try to sleep. They are such a nuisance, but when I see Mr Jarmon he will give me something to relieve them. You are not to look so worried, Renzo.'

'Naturally I am worried.' He came to her and taking her slender hands in his, carried them to his lips. 'You must stay with Jorja and myself until you are quite fit. I insist upon it, *madonnina*.'

She slowly smiled, and Jorja saw the velvety affection in her eyes, and the admiration of the Latin woman for a man who was every inch a man.

'I can see that marriage is agreeable for you, *caro mio*. I believe your charming English wife is good for your temperament.'

'I have temperament?' he mocked slightly, raising an eyebrow.

'From a small boy you have been very much

your own person.' The Contessa gazed from him to Jorja. 'No doubt you find my son something of a handful, eh? But if a woman is going to share her life with a man, then it is better most of the time that he should wear the trousers. Women, after all, have the nicer legs, have they not?'

Jorja glanced at Renzo and something seemed to clutch at her nerve centre when she thought of his hand travelling upwards from her instep, moving slowly along the slim length of her leg, tantalising her with his touch.

'I won't argue with that,' he said drily, and he reached down a hand and drew Jorja to her feet. 'We are going to leave you to take a rest, *madre*, and I think it might be a good idea for you to take a light lunch here in your bedroom.'

'*Si*, here among my lovely white flowers.' The Contessa smiled at Jorja. 'I will see you later, *cara*.'

'I'll look forward to it, *contessa*,' Jorja said warmly.

'I would much like it if you would call me *madre*, as Renzo does.'

'May I?' Jorja flushed, and felt Renzo's fingers tighten on hers.

'You are now my daughter by marriage.' The lady studied Jorja as she stood in conjunction with Renzo, her fairness as startling as his darkness. 'I would like to have been at the wedding, you know. Did you wear white, Jorja?'

'Yes.' Jorja wondered if her inward flash of pain showed in her eyes as she remembered standing at the altar with Renzo, feeling as if she were awake in a strange and forbidding dream. He had been but a proud-faced stranger to her; an angry man who forced her hand, taking hold of it with iron-hard fingers as he slid his ring into place. Right now she could feel the pressure of his fingers but she had learned that their caress could be more devastating than their cruelty.

'You must have looked very charming, my child.' The Contessa gave her son a reproving look. 'Do you think I am so frail, *caro*, that I would break into pieces to learn that you had exchanged one sister for the other. I am the mother of two strong-willed sons, who became a widow when I was thirty. I may look as if a wind would blow me over but women are deceptive. They have firm spines even if they lack muscle.'

'Then permit me to apologise, *madre*.' Renzo gave her a slightly grave smile. 'It would seem that men do have a tendency to misjudge women and I am no exception. Do you forgive me?'

'Not at this moment,' she retorted. 'You should have been married in Italy as Stelvio was, and we could have made it a family occasion. Renzo, *caro mio*, don't forget entirely that you are Italian, with old Roman blood beating through your veins. My Stelvio would never forget his heritage!'

The words stabbed through Jorja, and she almost gasped with pain as Renzo's fingers crushed hers. She bore the pain for moments on end, until he realised what he was doing and relaxed his grip on her, and as if to mask his feelings drew her fingers to his lips and kissed them.

'I don't forget my heritage, *madonnina*,' he said gravely. 'Maybe it is the things in the past which make of us the people we are. Just believe that I had your best interests at heart.'

'Very well.' His mother gave a slight shrug. 'I never pretended to know you as I always knew Stelvio. You were always in some respects an unknown quantity and marriage might make of you a man who shares his feelings a little more. Time will tell.'

'It is now time for you to rest.' He drew Jorja towards the door. 'We shall see you later, *madre*, and leave you in Cosima's good hands.'

As Jorja walked with Renzo to their own suite she could feel a trembling sense of rebellion in her body. 'It's so unfair,' she exclaimed. 'So wrong that your mother should put you in the dock!'

'What a very British way of putting it.' He quirked a look at her as they entered their sitting-room, then firmly he closed the door behind them and his hands drew Jorja towards him until they touched. He gazed down at her, searching the rebellious blue of her eyes. 'I believe you are hurt for me, *donna*.'

'Of course I am.' With a fingertip she ironed the tension from his face. 'Your mother's a lovely woman and I do understand why you don't want her to know all the facts relating to our marriage, but it is unfair that she should think of your brother as being a knight in radiant armour.'

'It is because of her fondness for him that I want those misconceptions of hers to continue.' Renzo tucked a strand of Jorja's fair hair behind her ear, his fingers lingering there to fondle her earlobe and the sensitive hollow behind it. 'You have seen for yourself that she is far from well, whereas I have a tough skin and I don't bruise easily.'

'Your bruises don't show,' Jorja murmured, 'but I know you have them.'

'Do you, child?' He bent his tall head and laid his lips lightly, then with a growing urgency upon hers. She surrendered to him instantly, aware of his need to salve those invisible hurts by the simple yet potent remedy of making love to her. Yieldingly she was his to undress and she saw the strain in his face giving way to a more primitive emotion as he took the straps of her slip in his fingers and slid them from her shoulders. As the silky fabric slithered from her body he held her between his hands and silently admired her.

Her pulses were racing madly, and when he spoke her name there was a slur in his voice . . . prelude to the unimaginable.

She gasped when he suddenly arched her over his arm and buried his face in her silky body. His lips roamed freely, and hazily she wanted to remind him to lock the door but she couldn't utter a word. He took her into the bedroom, laid her on the cool coverlet and with an almost savage impatience stripped off his clothing.

Her fingers gripped the smooth iron of his

shoulders and her body was an object of grace and invitation as she drew him close to her, forgetful of restraint, caring only that she bring him the solace he sought from her lips, drugged by his kisses as he took her with a totality that was painful until it became all at once a delirious pleasure.

Like this he was hers, every muscle of him, every black strand of hair, every far-reaching movement, as if with his body he reached into her heart and became part of its frantic beating. She held him, was possessed by him, and not even a shadow could have come between them.

Under the shower she found a love bruise on her left hip, just as Renzo entered the bathroom after making a call on the house telephone. 'Lunch in fifteen minutes——' There he broke off, came to her and kissed the bruising until she shuddered from the pleasure of his mouth on her skin.

'Lunch, remember?' She smiled shakily. 'We're having lamb chops and baby peas——'

Slowly he licked water from her skin. 'You are my lamb chop,' he murmured. 'With mint sauce sprinkled on you, you would be a feast.'

'You—we——' Her fingers were tangled in his hair. 'We must have some lunch.'

He raised his head and his smile travelled up her body, moving sensuously over its curves. 'In point of fact we are still on our honeymoon and entitled to live on lovemaking.'

'I know, but——'

'Are you shy, with my mother in the house?'

'I—I suppose I am,' she admitted. 'But I'm glad she's here, so we can take care of her.'

'What a very kind thing to say.' He wrapped his arms about her hips and rested his face against her. In the mirror Jorja could see their combined reflection, they looked like a sculpture of pagan lovers, welded together by the hand of fate.

'I really am quite hungry, Renzo.'

'Earthly wench.' He kissed her navel and rose to his feet. 'I suppose the *hors-d'oeuvre* has put an edge on your appetite?'

'I suppose it has,' she smiled, her eyes skimming his body.

'Renzo, we do share—something, don't we?'

'You are thinking of what *madre* said about me, eh?'

She nodded, and they entered the bedroom where she started to collect her scattered clothing. She felt an impulse to straighten the disordered bedcovers, but maids were employed to take care of the bedrooms, and she was well and truly entitled to be made love to in the middle of the day. Renzo might live in England but the tradition of the siesta was in his blood.

Her gaze stole around this room which was their sanctum, admiring the marvellous eighteenth-century bed upholstered in apricot silk and damask of a champagne colour. Beautifully carved posts were curtained in damask to the cornice, and there were fascinating dower chests on lion's-paw feet. One stood at the foot of the bed, the other against a wall, making Jorja think of the story of the bride who hid in such a chest and wasn't found until it was too late.

A shiver ran through her and she hastened with her dressing.

'You ask yourself too many questions.' Renzo buttoned his shirt and watched her as she slid her legs into silk stockings and fastened the little suspender buttons. 'When we are alone with each other we manage to be happy, don't we?'

'Yes, *signoresco*.' She knew what he meant, that physical passion enabled them to forget the fundamental facts of their marriage, but in the company of his mother they would be constantly reminded of Angelica's seduction of his brother. As she combed her hair at the mirror she couldn't help but see the apprehension in her eyes, replacing the excitement of a while ago when Renzo had been her wildly urgent, tawny-bodied lover.

Now when she turned to him, he looked remote but splendid in his well-cut ivory trousers and silky black shirt. She could see that his thoughts were no longer centred upon her, and it was hard to believe that it was less than an hour ago when his lips had kissed her so devouringly.

They went downstairs, wrapped in their individual thoughts, and ate at either end of a handsome rosewood table trailed by a sheath of white orchids. Their rack of lamb chops, each bone-tip dressed in a tiny white cap, was delicious. They were served wine in Venetian glasses with coiled serpent tails . . . and they didn't seem to know what to say to each other.

CHAPTER EIGHT

AFTERNOON tea was served in the garden room, upon a curled bamboo table, glass-topped for the tea-ware and cakes. The Georgian silver teapot was pear-shaped and the sunlight flickered in its chasing as Jorja refilled the Contessa's cup and her own. There was a selection of small sandwiches with delicious fillings, and a jam and cream layered sponge-cake, but neither of them felt like eating.

'*Grazie.*' The Contessa stirred her tea and her eyes dwelt on Jorja as she sat there with the sun on her hair. 'You are so blonde, *cara*, you would be lost in a wheatfield. *Una bionda bella.*'

Jorja smiled and tried not to show the anxiety she was feeling for Renzo's mother. After her visit to the specialist, and then various tests at the Regency Clinic, the decision had been made that she should undergo a bypass operation in order to relieve a badly blocked artery in her heart.

She was due to enter the clinic the following day and though she seemed composed, Jorja had noticed that her hands were a little unsteady.

'What a very English house this is, with a very English wife for my son,' she remarked, looking at ease in a dress of pale violet georgette upon the bamboo-framed chaise-longue. 'Renzo is very much a Latin, so it came as a surprise to me that he should want to settle in your country, *cara*. How do you enjoy being the wife of an Italian? Are you adjusting to—how shall I put it?—his masterful ways? He is not, and never could be, your average type of man.'

Jorja smiled at the very idea. 'I can only judge him against my father, who has devoted most of his time to his parish in Sussex. I looked after my father's house and had very little time left for a social life.'

'Meaning?' The Contessa raised a fine dark eyebrow above eyes intent upon Jorja.

'I had no men friends,' Jorja confessed. 'I am entirely a novice when it comes to dealing with a man. When I married Renzo I was as innocent, or almost, as a girl from a nunnery.'

The Contessa nodded to herself, as if unsurprised by what Jorja told her. 'It was a life your sister escaped from, eh? She wanted to be of the world?'

'Oh yes.' Jorja hoped she didn't reveal her sudden feeling of tension. All along it had been inevitable that Renzo's mother would want to discuss Angelica, whom she had met in Renzo's company and would have seen, as Jorja had, that her provocative beauty had got under his skin.

'So your sister chose to go on with her career as a fashion model?'

'Yes, *madre*.'

'And Renzo turned to you?'

Jorja nodded, and remembered vividly the day

of his proposal . . . as unexpected and piercing as the thorns he had removed from her hand.

'I can understand why he did so. Angelica struck me as being rather like a diamond which a man might want to flaunt, but you are more of a pearl. You have a silky fine lustre and you need to rest against a warm skin so your intrinsic self can be expressed.'

A tinge of amusement crept into the Contessa's eyes as a blush ran over Jorja's fair skin. 'Did you think I wouldn't notice that you respond, body and eyes, whenever my son is near you? A glow comes over you, as it overcomes a pearl when close to the warmth of its owner's skin—ah, you catch your breath, Jorja. Is that your Englishness taking affront at the idea of being owned by a man?'

'Perhaps,' Jorja admitted. 'I prefer to think that a marriage could be a deep friendship rather than a relationship based on possessiveness.'

'Latin men are possessive of their women, my child.' The amusement deepened in the elderly lady's fine eyes. 'Perhaps your sister reacted against that, as she has been the one to seek an independent life and a career. Do you think she did? After all, you must know her well as you grew up side by side. There cannot be that much difference in your ages—though obviously your experiences have been of a different kind. I had the impression that Angelica liked to be the centre of attention, but you would be happy to be the centre of Renzo's life, eh?'

'I—I would never be too clinging,' Jorja protested. 'He has his musical career and I realise that he has to give a good part of himself to his work. I would never interfere with that.'

'Ah, but don't be too self-effacing, *cara mia*. Men take advantage of that in a wife, and you must never permit yourself to be pushed into the background of his career. You are a charming young woman and you must be seen with him at the functions which he attends. You must overcome the shyness which your rectory life imposed upon you—if he had gone ahead with his marriage to Angelica, can you imagine that she would efface herself?'

Jorja shook her head, knowing in her heart just how far Angelica would go in order to be noticed.

'*Madre*,' her fingers pleated her lace-edged serviette, 'are you disappointed that Renzo married me?'

'Not disappointed,' his mother shook her head, 'but I am going to be candid and admit that I am surprised. Although my son Stelvio is two years younger than Renzo, he was the first to take a wife, an Italian girl of loveliness and character, of whom I am very fond. It seemed to me that Renzo was too wrapped up in his career and his business dealings and I would often ask him if he was ever going to settle down with a wife.'

The Contessa gave a very Latin shrug. 'He would placate me and say that one day, if he ever fell in love, he would relieve my anxiety that he would end up a bachelor, alone among possessions and without a son and heir. Then one day he came to Florence and your sister was with him. They were engaged and they seemed ideally suited, not only in looks but in their ability to walk into a room and be at once the centre, the focus of attention. They would never overpower each other. She would scintillate at his side, for at that time I believed Renzo needed that kind of a wife.'

The Contessa paused and seemed to consider her words as she studied Jorja. 'I believed he needed a public wife rather than a private one, as he has chosen to associate himself with the world of film-making, and when I met Angelica she seemed to have everything he could possibly need. You see, Renzo has never been, as boy and man, easy to estimate. He never had the spontaneous nature of my younger son and seemed to keep his feelings to himself. Consequently, I thought him proud and aloof, and I never made the attempt to delve into his personality.'

Again a pause and the Contessa rested her head against the cushions of the chaise-longue. Her gaze had drifted from Jorja to the garden and there was a reminiscent look in her eyes. 'I have always thought Renzo more clever, more talented than Stelvio, but he has never been so easy to love. Do I shock you, *cara*?'

'No.' Jorja spoke quietly, for she had shared the Contessa's opinion of Renzo . . . still, in some respects, shared an uncertainty about the man whose intimacy with her did not extend beyond the door of the bedroom. She, too, had felt him withdraw into a proud, hard shell when the kissing and the passion had been sated, and she had tried not to be hurt by him.

But love, she was discovering, was many-faceted and some of those facets had a chilling surface, as if it were wiser not to attempt to scale the peaks where in unseen chasms everything could be lost. She clung to what she had and didn't look upward at the glorious and dangerous heights.

Giddy heights, where on love's summit a person could see all the world and not want it because heaven was within reach.

'I think,' the Contessa murmured, 'that in our individual ways we both care for Renzo but find him elusive. Do you plan to have a child, Jorja?'

'I haven't made any plans,' Jorja smiled, 'but I shan't mind in the least if it happens.'

'I think your sister would have minded, eh?'

'Perhaps.'

'She has such a perfect figure and will want to retain it for as long as possible.' The Contessa indicated the delicious-looking jam and cream sponge which neither of them had yet touched. 'I am sure you haven't a care in the world about your figure, *cara*, and Renzo's cook might be offended if neither of us eats a slice of her cake. Do eat a slice and enjoy it for me. I confess to being a little nervous about tomorrow and I have no appetite, but you are young, and in love, I think, and love needs to be fed.'

'All right, you've tempted me.' Jorja took hold of the silver cake-slicer and the jam and cream oozed against the silver edge as she cut into the sponge-cake. From inside the house there was a sound of music, for Renzo was working on a theme for a new film, and Jorja suspected that he needed to work in order to keep at bay his anxieties about his mother's operation.

The specialist had been reassuring, but he had also made it plain that if the Contessa didn't have the operation she would become very ill and another attack might end her life.

'I expect you find life in London a whole lot different from life in the country, is that not so, Jorja? Noisier, faster, the very air tainted by the motor vehicles which pass back and forth through the city. You look to me as if you enjoy the green fields and the smell of smoke and apples in the autumn. You look the kind of girl who belongs among wheatfields rather than brick buildings, so being with Renzo must matter to you a great deal?'

'Yes, *madre*.' Jorja spoke the simple truth. In the beginning it had been a kind of nightmare, being forced by him to leave the green and pleasant hills of Duncton, but by some alchemy he made this Georgian house in London seem the only place that mattered. She could hear his music, share his life, and walk in the rooms and the garden which were his domain.

Renzo mattered more than she cared to admit, even to herself. Perhaps there was a primitive part of her that responded to the ruthless way he had made her a part of his life. Perhaps, secretly, she had wanted someone like him . . . or no one at all. Proud and defiant of the new rules which were being laid down by the feminists, who were contemptuous of women who dared to love a man who was master in the home and in the bedroom.

'You smile like the cat with the cream,' the Contessa murmured.

'This is very good sponge-cake.' Jorja still felt shy of revealing her feelings, though she sensed that the Contessa was in no doubt of them.

'Do you like to cook?'

'I was cook, housekeeper and gardener when I lived at home.' It still felt a little strange to Jorja that her days were no longer ruled by domestic tasks; that she had only to press a bell and a maid came to do her bidding. Leisure was a luxury she had never enjoyed before and she still had twinges of guilt about it.

'I expect your father misses you very much.' The Contessa spoke with a warm note of confidence in her voice.

'I——' Jorja bit her lip, 'I haven't heard from him since I married Renzo. He didn't attend our wedding—he thought it wrong of me to—to marry the man who had been engaged to my sister. Father adores her, you see. He has always wanted her to have everything she has ever wanted, but I—I didn't take Renzo away from her. I never dreamed that I would ever be his wife. It just—happened.'

'I think, *cara*, that you have permitted yourself to be overshadowed by Angelica.' A slight frown drew the lady's fine brows together as she took notice of Jorja's distress. 'You are a charming person in your own right, and I consider it unfair of your father to make you feel in any way guilty. Is Renzo aware of this?'

'Oh yes.' There swept over Jorja a painful re-collection of the scene which had taken place at the rectory; she sometimes felt that she would never forget how her father had reacted . . . as if she were breaking some unspoken vow never to be anything more than his unwed daughter. It hurt, deeply, that he should want her denial of all the pleasures which Angelica sought so greedily.

'You have gone far away in your thoughts, child.'

The attractive cadence of the Contessa's voice brought Jorja out of those disturbing realms where now and again she tried to find an answer to questions she dare not ask.

'I was thinking of Duncton, where my father's rectory is. I never thought to leave it, *madre*.' Jorja smiled with a touch of restraint. 'Life had taken on a pattern which seemed as if it would never change.'

'Then my Renzo threw a pebble in the pool, eh?'

'At the time it seemed more like a boulder,' Jorja laughed, a catch in her throat.

'You were overwhelmed, *cara*?'

'Totally.'

'You couldn't refuse him, eh?'

'He wouldn't let me.'

'Did you try to resist him?' His mother looked both amused and inquisitive, for the side that a mother never sees of her son is the one he presents to other women.

'I did try,' Jorja confessed. 'I believed—and still believe—that he has never forgotten Angelica.'

'My dear——'

'It's all right,' Jorja lied, 'I'm able to understand my sister's hold over men. When we were children and we used to dress up, she was always Fata Morgana and our mother made her one of those medieval hats with the veiling. I think she'll always be a heart-breaker.'

The Contessa gazed at Jorja in a fraught silence. 'Are you saying that your sister broke my son's heart?'

Jorja hesitated, seeing so vividly in her mind's eye the dark and passionate anger of his face when he had shown her the shameless letters which had spelled out in detail Angelica's pursuit of his brother.

'I believe she closed the door of his heart,' Jorja said quietly, 'and I sometimes think she is locked inside . . . as he believed her to be.'

'Believed her to be?' The Contessa leaned forward, her Latin eyes intent upon Jorja's face. 'What kind of a game has Angelica played with my son's feelings? There is more to all this than I've been told, is there not? What really happened between Renzo and your sister?'

A sudden anxiety gnawed at Jorja, for the Contessa held a hand to her left side, as if her palpitations had been set off by her need to get at the truth. She had to be soothed and led away from such a dangerous pursuit.

'Exactly what he told you.' Jorja spoke with a

composure she certainly didn't feel. 'Angelica has always been restless and inclined to leap from one enthusiasm to another in a short space of time. There's a difference between being a wife, especially to a man of Renzo's temperament, and being a fashion model always on show. Her enthusiasm for marriage suddenly left her; she couldn't give up the glamour of being a cover girl.'

'You will swear to that—that you are not hiding things from me? It would be like Renzo, with his secretive nature, and it's all too apparent that he can twist around his finger a young and inexperienced wife and make you do just what he wants. You would be no match for him—you might even be a little afraid of him.'

'I—I'm not——' Jorja denied. 'Truly, Angelica prefers the limelight to being a wife. Can you imagine Renzo allowing his wife to be photographed for the magazines?'

After a moment of thought his mother shook her head and leaned back against her cushions. 'But you think Renzo still cares for her—despite his marriage to you, *cara*?'

'Angelica is very beautiful——'

'Aren't you beautiful?'

'Not in her way.' Jorja shook her head, her hair glistening in the sunlight which made the garden room so pleasant, gently air-cooled as it was, and restful with its banks of green plants and the cool sound of the fountain playing upon the water of the fish pond.

'Her more apparent way, eh? Her awareness of

being attractive to men so that when she walks she moves her hip-bones a little more, and wears her clothes just a little tighter than you wear yours.'

Jorja gazed at Renzo's mother and realised that she had not been entirely fooled by Angelica, unlike the Reverend Michael who thought the sun shone out of her eyes.

'She has always been the outgoing one,' Jorja smiled, and tried not to remember to what extent Angelica had flaunted herself. It would be horrendous if their father ever learned of her activities in the world of show business. It would shatter all his fine-spun illusions about her, and Jorja feared that it would break him. When angels fell from grace, those who looked upon them as something special were the ones who suffered. There wasn't enough sensitivity in fallen angels for them to be damaged; it was their admirers, their lovers, and their doting fathers who limped away with their illusions badly bruised.

'I'm glad—pleased at the way things have re-arranged themselves.' The Contessa smiled to herself and seemed to be listening to the music which came in rich bursts, giving way suddenly to silences broken again by the melody which Renzo was matching to the mood of a film.

'Renzo has in his veins the Italian love of romantic music,' his mother said, her eyes velvety dark as she listened to what he was creating. 'Naturally I would have liked him to be a serious composer, one who would create sym-phonies, or operas in the style of Puccini, but he has a mind of his own and does only what it pleases him to do. Are you artistic in any way, Jorja?'

'I admire artistic people but I have no special talents, *madre*.'

'I think you may have a talent for creating repose,' the Contessa said thoughtfully. 'Have you noticed that Renzo uses his walking stick less and less? I believe he always had a dread that he would fall down in public and lose his Latin dignity, so the stick became a fixture with him. Now he begins to cast it aside, as if his inhibitions about his leg are no longer as manifest as they were. He has told you of his accident?'

'Only the barest outlines.' Jorja wanted to hear all she could about him; she wanted to make contact with the young Renzo, before he suffered physical trauma and had to cope with a damaged leg after having the full use of his body.

'Both my sons were extremely active, and they were also very competitive. They were racing against each other when the accident took place; their horses leapt the same obstacle and crashed head on. Renzo's mount went down and in its agony rolled on him until not a bone was left intact in his left leg. He was rushed into hospital and they wanted to amputate the leg, and it was only my obstinacy that made them rejoin the bones with steel pins, though the kneecap was beyond their skill to save.'

The Contessa spread her hands in a speaking gesture. 'Poor boy, he was in such pain for such a long time, and it was during that time that a change took place in him. He and Stelvio drifted apart, for the accident put years between them. No longer could they slam tennis balls at each other, leaping and running about the hard court, laughing and cursing each other in the light-hearted way of young men. No longer did they swagger into a ballroom and take for their dancing partners the most attractive girls there.

'From being a young man of physical activities, Renzo became a man of intellectual pursuits. He took up again the music he had lost interest in and there is no doubt that it helped him to bear the pain of his leg. I know there were times when he was furious with me; when he would have preferred an artificial limb to one that gave him no rest. But he and Stelvio were always handsome and full of the machismo which makes women go weak at the knees. I couldn't bear him to wear a prosthesis. I felt certain he had the tenacity to overcome the discomforts of his leg until it finally healed and became less of a burden to him, but in the process he changed. He grew into a man whom it became difficult to—know.'

The Contessa's eyes were sombre as she brooded upon her relationship with her eldest son. 'A mother does what she thinks best for her children, as you will discover for yourself, Jorja. I hope—pray that I shall live long enough to hold Renzo's child in my arms.'

'*Madre*——' Jorja knelt down by the chaise-longue and rested her cheek against the Contessa's thin hand, on which her rings seemed to weigh heavily, being of the type with wide gold bands embedded with gems. 'Your operation will give you a new lease on life. They perform miracles these days with all the new technology and know-how and in a very short time you'll be feeling on top of the world.'

'It would be nice to think so, *cara*.'

'You must believe so, *madre*,' Jorja spoke fervently. 'Having faith is half the battle, and you had it where Renzo was concerned. You knew he'd beat those devils that screamed in his leg day and night, and even yet they sometimes nag at him so they must have been fearful. I wish——'

Jorja paused, biting her lip and still shy of revealing her innermost feelings to anyone . . . those emotions which each day grew more intense, so that she almost feared their presence, budding and strengthening and thrusting their roots deep into her heart. It was almost as if love was a tree that grew inside people, spreading branches which could only grow strong and evergreen in the glow of a mutual love.

'What do you wish, *cara*?'

'That I could have been with Renzo when he was recovering from his accident. I—I should like to have held him and been able to comfort him a little. Pain is at its worst in the middle of the night, isn't it? I was only a schoolgirl when my mother died, but I remember how my father always kept a night-light burning beside her bed, and no matter how late the hour, he would softly read to her from one of her favourite books. Her door was always left ajar, so Angelica and I would hear his voice, reading or murmuring comfort, and in a way it comforted us to know she was never alone at night with her pain.'

Jorja sighed. 'That's how I remember my father, keeping vigil beside our mother until the night she quietly passed away. He came to our room and took us to see her at peace, and after that I've never been afraid of death. It's a long, quiet sleep, with no more anxieties, no more hurting, and I like to believe that our souls turn into birds, or maybe dragonflies, skimming over water with the sun shining through their wings.'

'How dare you discuss such a subject with my mother!' a voice rapped out from the archway into the garden room. 'Are you quite without a grain of sense, or too juvenile to realise what you're saying?'

Jorja slowly raised her head and gazed at Renzo in frozen surprise. He stared back at her with stone-hard displeasure, and once again they were like strangers, two people whose temperaments were only in tune when desire leapt and engulfed them in its flame. Now there was only the chill of his anger and it seemed to touch Jorja to the bone.

'I—I didn't realise——' she stammered.

'Renzo,' his mother sat up straight on the chaise-longue, 'your tone of voice is uncalled for. Look what you have done to Jorja, she has gone ash-white.'

'She has no right to introduce into this house, in your presence, a subject so *morboso*, and I have every right to chastise her for it. Death! Souls into birds! She's talking like a schoolgirl instead of a grown woman, and there are no excuses for her!'

The lash of his words drove Jorja to her feet. 'Excuse me!' She rushed blindly past Renzo out of the room, almost hating him for his own insensitivity. She knew he was worried about his mother and the operation tomorrow, but did he have to hurl abuse at her in order to relieve his tension? And if he had to hurl it, couldn't he have waited until they were alone?

Jorja glanced about her as if she didn't know which way to run. She didn't want to go upstairs to the suite which held too many reminders of him, and almost by chance she opened the door of the library, went quickly inside the book-lined room and closed the door behind her.

She leaned against the solid panels, counting the seconds until she felt certain he hadn't followed her. Only then did she sink down into a wing-backed chair, in the silence of a room where the passions of men and women were contained within leather bindings.

She could hardly believe that he had spoken so harshly to her in front of his mother, not at all like a man with a new wife, but like a man impatient with his marriage. He had surely undone all her attempts to make them appear happy, normal newly-weds. After all, it was what he had wanted, that his mother should believe they were in love and he had no regrets about his break with Angelica.

Jorja felt a bleakness edged by anger that he should treat her to such an outburst when all week long she had done her best to please him.

She shivered anew at the Latin ferocity of his attack, coming upon her so suddenly, in the midst of confiding to the Contessa the belief which had helped her to bear the loss of her own mother when she was a mere child.

Her fingers clenched the arms of her chair, for she couldn't give way to hurt feelings. They had to take second place to the ordeal awaiting her mother-in-law, whose frail body was due to go under the surgeon's knife.

Renzo's harshness had to be forgotten even if she couldn't quite forgive him. At times he seemed to want to crush out the idealism which set her apart from Angelica. As if the finer tuning of her system forced him to realise that their likeness was only skin-deep.

The remainder of the afternoon slid into evening and Jorja was dressing for dinner when Renzo appeared from his connecting room, not yet in his dinner-jacket, his eyes upon her as he fastened his grisaille cuff-links.

Jorja's body tensed inside her dress of opalescent silk chiffon as she waited for him to speak. 'Are you sulking?' he asked.

'Are you?' she retaliated, but in a quiet tone of voice which offered him no argument.

'What were you thinking of?' He crossed the room towards her and stood tall and dark above her slim and glimmering figure, the white linen of his dress-shirt intensifying the darkness which could always take her breath away. '*Madre* is unnerved enough without a discussion on the merits of dying. What gets into you, all those years of living in a house beside a churchyard?'

'Perhaps,' she admitted. 'But I didn't mean to add to your mother's state of nerves, I like her too much. It was to do with my father, the way he was with my mother, so kind and caring. I—I wouldn't set out to upset the Contessa for the world, and she didn't misunderstand me the way you did.'

Jorja turned away to the dressing-table and picked up one of her tiny drop earrings, quivering to the base of her spine when Renzo clamped her shoulders with his hands. 'I—don't want you to touch me,' she managed to say.

'So you are sulking, eh?'

'No.' She shook her head and held herself rigid. 'I won't quarrel with you, Renzo, because I realise how anxious you are feeling, but neither will I be snapped at and then have you lay hands on me as if nothing had happened. So let go of me, please.'

Instead he turned her to face him and with all the ease in the world pulled her into contact with him. Then he regarded her as if waiting for her to try and get loose, his eyes slightly narrowed as she stood in an attitude of cool reserve.

'I'm not going to put up with this,' he said at last. 'I think I had every right to be annoyed with you, and that annoyance is fast returning. I'm not in the mood tonight to have dealings with an adolescent wife, so I'd advise you, Jorja, to snap out of this silliness and be of some support to me. You know I'm worried as hell.'

'I know you are,' she said quietly, 'but shouting

at me in front of your mother doesn't help the situation. I—I had hoped to convince her that we're all right together.'

'Aren't we?' he interjected.

Jorja stood physically close to him but for once his closeness didn't excite her; she remained too aware of her lacerated feelings. 'The only time we achieve any harmony is when we're—there.' She made a graphic gesture towards the bed, shrinking inside at having made herself say the words.

He stared towards the bed and his face showed the bone-structure beneath the skin. The bed was made up for the night, with the lamps agleam at either side of it. The canopy reared above the wide comfort they had shared, locked in each other's arms. He hadn't abraded her then, with a voice hard as nails, or called her a juvenile without a grain of sense. He had thoroughly enjoyed himself with her, and a crushing kind of heat seemed to envelop Jorja as she remembered the intensity of his passion, making her feel as if she had to get out of this room, away from him.

'That's all you've wanted of me, ever since Sandbourne,' she said breathlessly. 'Every hour we've ever spent together has been no more than gratification for you, then you want to turn your back on me. You want to forget that I'm your wife, and this afternoon you really forgot it! You spoke to me as if I'm nobody, cutting me down to size as if all the time we've spent making love has left you feeling nothing for me—nothing!'

Her eyes blazed into his, the sheerest of blue,

like that at the very centre of a flame. 'Oh God, I wish I could leave you tonight, Renzo, but we —we both know I can't. Your brother should be here, to share what's going to happen to your mother tomorrow, but instead I'll stay and share it for her sake. You—your brother—I believe you're both cut from the same cloth. I don't believe there's a scrap of difference between you —you competed as young men, but then it was horses and tennis. Now it's Angelica, isn't it? You've both shared her!'

The words seemed to bounce back and forth against the walls of the room, loud in Jorja's head, but not quite so loud as the sudden rap on the bedroom door and the entrance of Torrence. 'Begging your pardon, sir, but you are wanted at once in the Contessa's room. The poor lady is very unwell——'

Renzo had departed almost before Torrence had ceased speaking, and Jorja rapidly asked the butler if the doctor had been sent for. He shook his head. 'We thought it best that the *signore*——'

'It's all right, Torrence.' Jorja went to the telephone in the sitting-room and dialled the number which she had memorised days ago, just in case of an emergency. It was the home number of Sir Ronald Jarmon and thankfully he was there, a sigh of resignation in his wife's voice when she said they had been about to take dinner. She called him and he came on the line, and Jorja repeated that her mother-in-law was feeling unwell.

'I'll come at once.' There wasn't any hesitation in his voice, and Jorja felt a sinking feeling inside her. She cradled the receiver and when she turned from the telephone, Torrence was still hovering in the doorway.

'We were all hoping, madam, that the Contessa would keep up her strength until tomorrow,' he murmured, and no longer did he regard Jorja as on the day of her arrival at Hanson Square, as if she were young and callow and unused to responsibility.

'I was praying for it,' she rejoined. 'With her heart in such a shaky condition she can't afford setbacks——' Jorja broke off as Cosima came hurrying into the room, her face greatly distressed as she caught Jorja by the arm.

'You must come,' she said distractedly. 'The Contessa wants you—come!'

Jorja barely remembered her arrival in the Contessa's bedroom, where her mother-in-law was propped up by pillows, her lips the violet colour of the dress she had worn at teatime. Renzo was beside her, holding and chafing her hands as if to warm them, and when Jorja came quickly to the bedside he gave her a look she wouldn't forget—the agonised look of a man who found himself in a situation he couldn't control.

'*Cara bella*.' A little light flickered in the old lady's eyes when she caught sight of Jorja, and with an effort she withdrew a hand from the clasp of Renzo's hands and reached out to her. The feel of the tremulous, icy-cold fingers almost made

Jorja cry out. No! *Madre* had to hold on so the operation could take place. It would make her well again and she wouldn't have these seizures which left her fighting for breath.

'Spare yourself, *madre*,' she pleaded. 'The doctor is on his way to you a-and soon you'll feel better——'

'With no more hurting, eh?' The Contessa had her eyes fixed upon Jorja's face, her breath dragging back and forth among the words she wanted to say. 'It was good we talked—*contento, cara. Contento.*'

Jorja felt her throat closing up with tears, and silently she nodded and allowed her hand to be drawn in the direction of Renzo's. She could see that his mother had now gone beyond speech but in this way she asked Jorja to contend with the difficulties of loving him, the son who had always been more aloof than Stelvio but who was with her now. Her final awareness must have been of their three hands meeting, then came a groan of protest from Renzo, and the sound of Cosima weeping distractedly.

It was over and Jorja stood there in the throes of painful memory, her hair haloed by the lamplight as she leaned down and kissed the Contessa's cheek, the fine skin already cool beneath the touch of her lips, the far distances of death between them.

'I loved you, *madre*. I'm glad we met.'

When she raised her head she met Renzo's eyes and they were like diamonds set deep in a pitiless pain.

'Leave me alone with my mother,' was all he said, and taking Cosima by the arm, Jorja did as he asked.

CHAPTER NINE

JORJA realised that it was deep-felt anger with his brother which made Renzo decide to have his mother buried in an English cemetery.

'To the devil with Stelvio!' he said furiously. 'He repays *madre*'s love by being elsewhere when she had most need of him. Well, it's over and now I'll see to it that she is laid to rest in this country. Here, where I make my home!'

He chose a beautifully kept cemetery at Richmond and set about making his arrangements for the funeral while his mother's body lay in a chapel of rest, her casket blanketed in gorgeous white flowers, those blooms which she had always loved so much. They filled the small chapel with their scent, the tinted light of the chapel windows softly colouring them.

The casket looked so tiny to Jorja, who went alone to the chapel to pray for *madre*, and to remember her own mother. As she knelt there on a red cushion, she breathed in the atmosphere of the place and felt in no awe of death. Despite Renzo's anger with her that last day of his mother's life, she was glad that she and *madre* had talked of things important to them.

Perhaps without knowing it they had both felt a premonition of what was going to happen, the evening of that sunlit day. Jorja was thankful that it had been a lovely day, and even more deeply thankful that the Contessa had not suffered for hours. The attack had come quickly, Cosima had told her. The Contessa had been combing her hair at the dressing-table while Cosima laid out her dress for dinner. All at once she had risen from the dressing-stool and had started across the room . . . she had cried out something Cosima couldn't remember, then in the act of falling had been saved by her companion, who carefully lowered her to the floor. Thinking that a drop of brandy would revive the Contessa, Cosima had rung for Torrence, who after taking one look at the collapsed woman had fetched Renzo to her.

It was Renzo who had carried his mother to the bed and propped her among pillows in an effort to ease her rapid breathing. It had all been over within half an hour, and later Sir Ronald Jarmon had confirmed heart failure.

Jorja approached the open casket and gazed down at the peaceful face of the woman whose friendship she would have valued so much. She was far away now, sleeping the long, unbroken sleep there among the white flowers, her lovely, chiselled head resting upon an ivory satin pillow.

Snapping off the head of a white carnation, Jorja placed it in her handbag. She had pleaded with Renzo to try and get in touch with Stelvio, but with a jaw like iron he had refused to make the effort. According to Monica, who would be arriving from Italy in a few hours, Stelvio was somewhere in the Adriatic, cruising on the yacht of a friend and, obviously, still in the company of Angelica.

'I told you,' Renzo's eyes had not lost their diamond hardness, 'I wish him in hell before I'll lift a finger to beckon him to *madre*'s funeral. I thank the saints she never found out about his philandering, and so far as I'm concerned he can go to the bottom of the sea with his *puttana*.'

Jorja had to leave it there, for it was hopeless, trying to reason with Renzo in his present state of mind. His mother's death had affected him deeply and he didn't want to listen to anyone. His mind was made up. The Contessa was going to be buried in England instead of the old family vault in Italy, and when Jorja pointed out that it might have been her wish to be with her husband, Renzo made a curt gesture with his hand.

'He died long ago; his body was ashes when recovered from the wreckage of his plane. He had a woman with him! Her name was never known and her ashes mingle with his in the family vault, so you can spare me your sentimental idea that *madre* should repose there!'

Jorja walked through the small park near the chapel and was waiting to hail a taxi to take her home when a steel-grey Porsche drew into the kerb beside her. She gave the car a startled glance when the passenger door was opened. 'Jump in!' a voice invited. 'You remember me, don't you? I'm the chap who handed you over to another man.'

'Bruce!' She couldn't keep a note of warmth and relief out of her voice, and no longer hesitant she slid into the car and relaxed into the seat at his side. 'How nice to see you.'

'I'll second that.' He ran his eyes over her face, which showed some of the strain she had been feeling for the past few days. 'I was sorry to hear about Renzo's mother. She was a gracious lady.'

Jorja nodded. 'I knew her for only a short while and just as we were becoming friends, and we were all so hopeful about the operation, she collapsed.'

'When I heard the news from Flavia and phoned Renzo to offer my condolences, I could tell how hard it had hit him.' Bruce started the car and drove into the stream of traffic. 'I asked if he was flying his mother's casket home to Italy and he informed me that the funeral is taking place at Richmond on Friday.'

'He's quite determined,' Jorja said quietly, 'and it's no use trying to reason with him because he doesn't listen to me. He's made no attempt to contact his brother and refuses to even try. I'm afraid when Renzo sets his course, nothing short of a cyclone stops him.'

'True,' Bruce murmured. 'I happen to know what the bone of discord is between him and Stelvio; I know it's to do with your sister.'

'I—I'm rather glad that you know,' Jorja admitted. 'It makes things easier.'

'Between us, Jorja?'

'Yes.' For the first time in days Jorja felt some of the tension easing out of her system. Being in Renzo's presence had been like waiting for Vesuvius to erupt; grief, anger and bitterness smouldering in him like hot lava that might at any moment reach boiling-point.

'In need of a confidant?' Bruce asked. 'I can be an understanding chap, so don't hesitate to make use of me. Look, I'm on my way to a lonely lunch so how about joining me? You don't have to hurry home, do you?'

'N-no.'

'That's great.' He sounded so pleased that Jorja found herself glancing at him in surprise. He was an attractive man and she felt certain the women in his life were the stunning and exotic actresses whom he directed. She wondered how well he had known Angelica, and whether he was aware of the more sensational aspects of her career.

'I can't imagine you eating a lonely lunch,' she said.

'Can't you?' He turned the Porsche into a side road leading away from the heavy traffic. 'Do you think I'm always surrounded by glamorous film stars?'

'A lot of the time, I bet.'

'Too much of the time,' he said wryly. 'Put a man in a hothouse among orchids and it isn't too long before he's panting for fresh air and clover. From seven onwards I've been trying to shoot a scene with Amanda Miles, and believe me it's been hair-raising. On screen she looks heavenly, but everything she's got is on the surface and she can forget her lines quicker than a seal can eat sardines. Believe me, Jorja, being with you is like peace after chaos. The very look of you in that cool grey suit is soothing.'

A smile dented Jorja's mouth, and then was gone. She felt sure that most women would like to be told that they looked exciting, but she understood what Bruce meant. Her spirit had been in something of a turmoil and she felt soothed by his company.

'Where are we going to lunch?' she asked.

'At a favourite restaurant of mine, The Silk Lantern in Chelsea. I favour good cuisine rather than gilt cupids and palm trees and the sight of corporation bosses fishing for business, like the merchants in the temple. You'll like where we're going.'

'I'm sure I shall.' She traced with a fingertip the crocodile markings of her handbag. 'Are you coming to the funeral, Bruce?'

'Yes, I'd like to attend. In a way, I don't really blame Renzo for choosing her place of rest in England. He's here more often than he's in Italy, and it's comforting to be able to take flowers to a memorial stone. Is Monica Talmonte attending?'

'She's arriving from Italy today.' Jorja bit her lip in thought, hoping there wouldn't be too much constraint in meeting Stelvio's estranged wife. She was leaving their little girl at home with her governess and intended to stay at Hanson Square for only a couple of days. Jorja looked forward to the meeting, but sensed that it wasn't going to be an easy one. She, after all, was Angelica's sister.

'Are you feeling apprehensive?' Bruce asked.

'I'm afraid so.'

'You mustn't, you know, feel too responsible

for other people's feelings, Jorja. You'd be surprised how basically tough and resilient most people are, and I don't think it altogether wise to be over-sensitive, least of all where love is concerned.'

'That sounds rather cynical, Bruce, yet I don't think you are a cynic.'

'Let's say I'm cautious,' he rejoined. 'I live and work in a world where love is lucky if it lasts a week, and I've been part of that world since I was sixteen. I'm the boy who worked his way up from odd-jobbing to being the guy who calls the tune, and on my way I've met a variety of characters, some of them charming, others monstrous, and most of them ambitious. Be guided by me, keep a picket fence around your heart and be a little more detached about people. It pays off and the dividend is that you don't get hurt.'

'It's probably sound advice, Bruce, but a little late in my case.' And a little too late to recall a remark which, as he parked the car, had him turning in his seat to look at her intently.

'Is Renzo hurting you?' he wanted to know.

'Not intentionally—at least, I don't think so.' She forced a smile but could see he wasn't fooled. 'He—shuts me out, emotionally, and I suppose I've always believed that marriage means communication on all levels.'

'Why did you marry him?' Bruce asked, and he leaned a little nearer to her. 'No bride ever looked as you did, as if everything that was happening was unreal—Renzo most of all. I handed you over to him, but I should have snatched you out

of that church before the vows were spoken and
he put that ring on your finger.'

Bruce took hold of her left hand and studied the
gemmed ring. 'He applied some kind of pressure,
didn't he? Ah, I know you won't tell me, but I've
always been aware that there's a devilish side to
Renzo, and a girl like yourself wouldn't be any
match for him if he used fascination or force.
Which was it?'

'A combination of both,' she found herself
admitting. 'There was no way I couldn't marry
him even though I knew he still—wanted
Angelica.'

'My dear girl——' Bruce's fingers tightened on
hers. 'It's no situation for you to be in, not in this
day and age. Not if Renzo keeps you with him out
of sheer perversity.'

'Oh, there's more to it than that.' She could feel
herself flushing and looked away from him,
avoiding his eyes. 'I'm longing for my lunch
—shall we go in?'

He held her hand a moment longer, then released it. 'I didn't know,' he murmured, 'that
girls like you could still be found. I had begun to
believe that they were all wrapped up in tinsel
and self-interest.'

'I—I suppose I'm old-fashioned.' Jorja slid
from the Porsche and after Bruce had locked the
car, they went across the road to where the restaurant stood two storeys high on a corner, the
aroma of good food greeting them as they entered. Bruce had a regular table on the second
floor, above stairs that curved around into a large,

vintage dining-room where the silk lanterns cast a soft orange glow over the spotless tables.

'This is nice!' Jorja exclaimed.

'I certainly think so.' This time Bruce captured her gaze as they were seated at his table beside a window. 'What would you like to drink?'

'May I have a tawny port?' A smile crept into her eyes. 'Old-fashioned, as I said.'

'I'll join you in your choice.' He turned to the waiter. 'Mario, this is a rare young woman who refuses to be swept back and forth by the changing tides of what is in vogue. Tawny port for both of us.'

The waiter inclined his head and handed them their menus. 'We have a particularly fine blend, Mr Clayton, which I feel sure the young lady will enjoy.'

'She needs some solace as well, Mario, for there's a bereavement in her family.'

'Ah, my commiserations, madam!'

'Thank you, you're kind.' Once again Jorja decided that she liked this place and its atmosphere, and was glad she had run into Bruce. Yes, it was nice to receive solace, and much as she had tried to give it to Renzo, he had turned a hard, aloof shoulder and made it difficult for her to approach him.

'Now what do you fancy?' Bruce was studying the menu. 'The Dublin Bay prawns are always delicious, like lobster tail-meat. Or how about fillets of trout with a parsley sauce?'

'What are you having, Bruce?' She felt like being a little helpless today, indulging the loneliness which had come over her in the past few days.

'I'm inclined to go for the prawns.' He glanced at her over the menu-card, a smile touching his mouth but leaving an intent green light in his eyes. 'With a green salad and black pepper, eh?'

She nodded, and studied the main dishes. 'Pot-roast chicken,' she murmured. 'I haven't had that since I—I left home. Daddy and I would make a fuss of ourselves if one of his parishioners gave him a chicken. I love it with dumplings and carrots.'

When Bruce didn't reply, she glanced at him and saw a look on his face which made her eyes widen with enquiry. 'Do you think I'm terribly naïve?' she asked. 'Still the girl from the rectory whom Renzo finds boring?'

Bruce slowly shook his head. 'If Renzo doesn't appreciate your charm and candour, then let me take over,' he said deliberately. 'Why didn't I ever ask Angelica to introduce us?'

Jorja's fair skin couldn't hide or control a blush. 'If she mentioned me at all, then she probably made me sound like the typical spinster, content with her lot. It wouldn't be cattiness on her part, because I was unstirred by men. Even after she brought Renzo to the rectory, I didn't realise until later that he had—got under my skin.'

'Too deep for removal?'

Her fingers clenched the menu-card. 'We shouldn't be talking like this——'

'Perhaps we were meant to talk like this from the moment we met.'

'No.' She denied him with a shake of her head. 'You're Renzo's friend—I'm Renzo's wife—and you were there in church when we took each other for better or worse.'

'And you'll stand by that, even though you know how he still feels about your sister?'

'I knew how he felt on the day he proposed to me.' The old pain, and some of the rebellion darkened her blue eyes, and for a few moments they sat in silence while their port was poured. Then almost in unison they lifted their glasses and drank from them. The port was warming, wending its way through Jorja as if seeking to carry that warmth to her heart.

'What was he after?' Bruce demanded. 'Some way to get back at Angelica, and you, Jorja, the weapon he used?'

She couldn't look at Bruce, for the answer to his question was there in her eyes and there was no hiding it.

'Damn him to blazes,' Bruce muttered, for his former tone of voice had turned a couple of heads at a nearby table. 'I knew he could slam the gates of mercy if it suited him, but it's unforgivable of him not to give a damn for your feelings. Surely he can see that you have feelings Angelica hasn't even heard about?'

'Our feelings aren't always selective, are they?' She sipped her port, and her body at least had lost that chill which had set in ever since the evening of the Contessa's death. That was when Renzo had withdrawn from her; that was when he had stayed the night long in his mother's room, so that not until the morning had the men from the funeral parlour been allowed to remove her body from Hanson Square.

Unshaven, far from everyone in his thoughts, Renzo had walked in the garden alone. Then later, shaved and groomed again, he had come to her and told her of his decision to have his mother interred in an English cemetery. Argument had been hopeless. He had brushed it away as if it were a troublesome fly. 'It's my business,' he told Jorja. 'I don't need to consult you or anybody else.'

It was during their course of Dublin Bay prawns that Bruce asked Jorja a direct question. 'Do you love him?'

Jorja applied butter to brown bread, and was confused by her inability to give him a direct answer. Hurt, yes. Bewildered, and certainly bothered, but only when she was in Renzo's arms and desire had its grip on him, excluding everything but the physical, did she feel any sense of security. When the moment came to release her from his arms, she was on her own again, the link between them fraying at the edges, tearing and letting go as the desire ebbed away. Even his tone of voice would change. Gone, that seductive murmur of a man enthralled by the shape and feel of her.

'He's like Janus,' she said, in a troubled voice. 'He has two faces and I don't know which is the reality.'

'You mean,' Bruce frowned and ran his eyes over her face and hair, both so fair and somehow innocently untouched despite her marriage, 'he has a night face, and a daytime one. It figures! He'd have to be a cold fish if he didn't take advantage of a lovely thing like you!'

'Bruce!' She flushed vividly. 'Please don't——'

'By God,' he showed his white teeth, 'I'd give anything to have you saying *please do*.'

'Bruce——'

'Yes,' he leaned forward, holding her distressed eyes, 'I'd like to spoil you like mad, and make you realise just how much a man can care —if he has the right girl to care about. Jorja, you deserve a whole-hearted man, not just his attentions when it's bedtime. All right, I know that sounds crude, but it's the truth, isn't it?'

'I—I don't know how we got around to having this conversation, so can we stop it?' She looked at him defiantly, and found her gaze on his mouth. A good, firm mouth, slightly moist from the big, delicious prawns. No one, not even Renzo, had ever spoken as if she mattered for herself alone. As if she were worth lifting on to the kind of pedestal her sister had always enjoyed, her favours sought with adoring eagerness.

'If we stop now,' Bruce said, 'we may never find another opportunity to begin again.'

'That may be for the best,' she retorted.

'And is it for the best that you go on being the key which Renzo keeps twisting in the locked gates of his heart?'

She winced, for the words conjured up iron resistance to all her tender needs . . . to see Renzo look at her from across a room, as if not an atom of distance divided them. It could never happen, for when he looked at her, the slim, golden figure of Angelica glided between them . . . the lovely and insidious serpent in any garden they tried to plant with the seeds of love.

'Perhaps, Bruce, you've lived and worked too long in a world where people walk out on their responsibilities if they don't happen to bring them a constant source of happiness or pleasure. The film world isn't renowned for constancy, is it? It's in the world of reality that people have to come to terms with their lives, and that's what I have to do.'

'You're a sweet-faced fool, Jorja.'

She dabbed her lips with a serviette. 'Those prawns were enjoyable.'

'I'm glad our table-talk hasn't ruined your appetite.'

'Renzo was working on the new music just before—anyway, it sounded beautiful to me. It sounds as if the film is a very romantic one.'

'A romantic drama.' Bruce sat back in his chair and considered her, a half-quizzical gleam in his eyes. 'Thank heaven we managed to get ourselves a real actress for that one, because it happens to be one of the rare women's films made these days. Renzo put up half the money, did you know?'

'Did he really?' Her eyes lit up. 'Then he must have a great deal of faith in the story; he's no one's fool when it comes to hard cash, is he?'

Their empty dishes were whisked away and

their main meal was served. As Jorja breathed the aroma of her pot-roasted chicken and watched the fluffy dumplings being added to her plate, she had an irresistible image of the rectory dining-room, with its embossed wallpaper, oak table and high-backed chairs. A homesick feeling swept over her and she decided to telephone her father when she arrived home at Hanson Square. They couldn't go on being distant with each other, for life could end so suddenly, and regrets weren't easy to live with.

'So Monica arrives some time today?' Bruce sliced into his steak.

'Yes. Renzo's going to the airport to pick her up, and I must admit I'm a little bit nervous about meeting her.'

'Naturally enough. There's bound to be a bit of tension, but as I've already advised you, pet, stand back and try to be detached. You aren't, after all, your sister's keeper.'

'But she has been responsible for hurting Monica.'

'Look,' Bruce waved his fork at her, 'don't go turning yourself into a whipping-girl for Monica as well as Renzo. Your sister's damnable sins aren't yours—I doubt if you could commit a sin if you tried, and that's half your trouble.'

'What do you mean, Bruce?' She gave him a startled look across her plate of chicken.

'Martyrs get strewn with ashes not flowers, Jorja. Someone hands them a cross to carry, not a bunch of roses. You're a pretty nice person, but it worries me the way you allow your niceness to be used as a whiplash. You aren't being fair to yourself.'

'I—I can only be the person I am.'

'True, and the person you are deserves to emerge from its cocoon of concern for others and their wretched problems. Live, laugh and be merry, pet, because if you take on the cares and woes of those around you, they'll selfishly assume that it's what you like, what you prefer.'

Jorja ate in silence, absorbing his words. They rang with a truth she couldn't deny, for hadn't her father assumed that she had no need of carefree pleasures and was content to be burdened with a big old house and coping with parishioners who came knocking on the side door, woeful with problems she was expected to solve.

Strangely, she hadn't noticed how much of her time and trouble had been expended on others, so that in looking back she seemed not to remember the dream years between adolescence and becoming an adult. There was no time for experimenting with hairstyles and clothes; no time to dream of a potential lover. Someone had to see to things, or the three of them would have been living in a house of cobwebs, surviving on cheese sandwiches.

'Bruce,' she smiled ruefully, 'it would seem that I'd suit everyone better if I had my sister's ways. You, Renzo—my father.'

'Good lord, I'm not saying that——'

'You are, you know.' She drank from her wine glass. 'Be less caring, you're telling me. Live for yourself and let others flounder around in their problems. Angelica does all that, and leads everyone a merry old dance in the process. The *femme fatale*, whom few men can resist. Well, she was born that way and can't help herself. I was born my way and I can't help it if I have a foolish heart.'

In an almost painful silence Bruce gazed across the table at Jorja, taking in her air of quiet strength, lightly touched with a humorous acceptance of devils and angels.

'You know what I'd like?' he breathed. 'I'd like to come round to you, grab you in my arms, and never let you set foot in Renzo's house ever again. I've never wanted any girl as madly as I want you, and you've said yourself that he wants Angelica.'

'Oh—you mustn't say such things——' There were shadings of distress and a tinge of wonderment in her wide blue eyes. She had missed the fun of flirtation in her formative years, making her realise why she couldn't fully cope with men, even though now she was married to an aloof, complex Latin who could also be breathtakingly passionate.

'Don't you like it?' Bruce stroked his green eyes over her face. 'Doesn't it excite you in the smallest degree that we're together in my favourite restaurant and no one knows we're here, and saying these things to each other? Come, wouldn't you be less than honest if you said no?'

'I—shouldn't be here, Bruce. I should be at home, making sure everything is being prepared for Monica's arrival.'

'Forever duty-bound,' Bruce mocked. 'Forever

concerned to put other people's needs before your own. You're unbelievable, do you know that?'

'I might seem so to you.' She laid her knife and fork side by side on her plate. 'You've told me that the women you know are wrapped up in themselves.'

'I haven't known all of them intimately,' he said drily. 'They may have hidden virtues, but at this moment all I see, all I care about is a girl I gave away to another guy. I'd like to twist the arm of fate for doing that to me.'

'We were strangers,' she pointed out. 'Everything was strange to me that day. None of it was tangible and all I knew was that I was saving Daddy from being hurt——'

She broke off, but it was too late to bite back her words. She saw the comprehension leap into her companion's eyes. She could see that with a half-sentence she had told Bruce everything.

'So that was it?' He set his jaw grimly. 'Renzo was going to spill the beans relating to your sister's affair with his brother, unless you married him and made it look as if he didn't give a damn. It didn't matter what happened to your pride so long as his didn't suffer—Jorja, how can you stay with a man like that?'

How often she had asked herself such a question, but from the beginning half of her had resisted Renzo while the other half had discovered at Sandbourne that when he touched her, when he laid his warm and coppery body close to hers, she was lost to all reasoning. The answer was that she was in thrall to Renzo in a physical way, and Bruce could only see that outwardly she looked a cool, fair English girl whose lips, whose skin and eyes didn't reveal any of the tumultuous feeling which Renzo could arouse in her.

No matter how passionate the lovemaking, the memories alone were left when it was over; the features of the face and the lines of the body didn't reveal the emotions or the ecstasy. They remained the secret of the senses.

'Do any of us,' she asked, 'do anything that we don't truly want to do? Perhaps in the subterranean passages of our psyche we follow blindly the false lights of our secret desires.'

'Are you saying, Jorja, that you secretly desired your sister's fiancé?'

'Does it seem so impossible?' Her smile wasn't fully realised. 'I was a girl whose world was bounded by rectory walls, and the hills and dales of Duncton. In bed I read of the imperious men inside the books of the Brontës and Jane Austen, and one fine day my beautiful sister walked into the rectory parlour with a man who looked as if he had stepped out of *Pride And Prejudice*. He wore the most perfect suit, and when he was introduced to me, he kissed my hand.'

She paused and her smile shook slightly at the edge of her mouth. 'Does it seem so strange, Bruce, that I was a fish struggling on his hook even before he landed me?'

'What became of the hook?' Bruce growled. 'Isn't it still sticking in your lovely flesh?'

She quivered, and a ray of sunlight made her hair shimmer. She sat there in silence as their waiter cleared the table and asked if they would like the dessert trolley to be brought to their table.

'I—I don't think I could manage a sweet,' she said. 'My lunch was perfect——'

'Take a look at the trolley anyway,' Bruce coaxed. 'The chocolate ice-cream gâteau is a marvel; just wait till you see it.'

'All right, you've weakened my resistance,' she smiled, meeting the eyes of this man who had coaxed out of her things she had never meant to say. She felt a stab of compunction. Renzo might not love her, but he trusted her. Everyone had always trusted her.

As Bruce had promised the gâteau was marvellous and they both enjoyed a slice of it, followed by coffee. 'What,' Bruce asked, 'are we going to do about us?'

'Nothing,' she said simply. 'We met, we lunched, and on Friday you'll attend the funeral and forget we talked like this.'

'Would that be the way of it—if you didn't have that ring on your finger?' he asked.

Jorja glanced at the ring, its gemmed beauty glinting against her fingers. What, she wondered, would she be feeling if she had met Bruce Clayton while she was still living at home at Duncton? She quite honestly felt that she would have been attracted to him, but doubted if he could ever have been as ruthless as Renzo had been in prising her out of the rectory, which like a shell had grown around her until she couldn't imagine life without it.

'Tell me to my face that you don't enjoy my company,' he persisted.

'I—I enjoy it very much,' she admitted, 'but nothing can change the fact that I'm married to Renzo. I don't live in your kind of a world, Bruce, where people cast off each other as if, like coats, they had lost their warmth. You mustn't make the mistake of thinking that because I look rather like Angelica I think like her, and can behave like her. She suits herself and isn't really aware of other people's feelings.'

'Aren't you aware of mine, Jorja?'

'Oh, I just think you're a little bored and disillusioned by the women you have known.'

'Knowing them has at least shown me what I've been missing.'

'Well, now you know what to look for, a girl from the country who prefers to see fur coats on the rabbits, and the sun sparkling on a stream to the biggest diamond in Bond Street.'

'So you're going to pass up the chance to be the light of my eyes?'

'You've kissed the Blarney Stone, Mr Clayton.'

'I want, madly, to kiss you.'

'Please, play fair.'

'Love was never a game that could be played by the rules. Hasn't your sister broken every one of them? Hasn't she pitted brother against brother, and yet has the pair of them in love with her? You must face reality, Jorja. Any time Angelica wants Renzo again, your feelings won't matter a brass farthing. They never did matter to her, did they? And I suspect that they never really mattered to him.'

Jorja flinched from the sting of his words; he was saying things that she had said over and over to herself, but hearing them spoken aloud was unutterably painful.

She glanced at her wristwatch. 'I have to be getting home, Bruce. I've enjoyed every mouthful of my lunch, and I've especially liked The Silk Lantern.'

'I usually come here alone, so feel flattered.'

'I feel privileged.' She watched as he settled the bill, noticing the clean strength of his hands as he refolded his wallet and put it away.

As she rose from her chair, he was there beside her and for a moment their eyes met and she was almost tempted to blurt out that she was dreading the aftermath of the funeral, when Renzo had to come to terms not only with grief but with the possible regret of not having his brother with him at the graveside. The words almost broke the bounds of her restraint, then she hurried ahead of Bruce down the stairs that led to the street.

'I think,' she tried to speak casually, 'that it might be better if I went home in a cab.'

'You'll do nothing of the sort.' He took her firmly by the arm and led her across to the small car-park where his car waited. 'What are you afraid of, that I'm going to kiss you?'

'You mustn't——' She gazed at him uncertainly; the sun had gone behind a cloud and her face had a pensive look.

'Why,' Bruce touched a hand to her waist, 'afraid you might like it too much?'

She drew away from him and slid quickly into the Porsche. His firm body had touched hers and again she had felt a traitorous longing to give in to nervous uncertainty and the need to be sheltered against the storms of her marriage. She might, indeed, enjoy his kisses, for she had learned in Renzo's arms that she had a responsive nature and a deep need for affection.

With Bruce she might discover the affection, for in his embrace she would be Jorja; she would be herself and not a substitute for Angelica.

Never had temptation felt so strong, and Jorja knew that other women in her shoes would have turned to Bruce and asked softly to see where he lived.

'Well, Jorja,' there was a note of tension in his voice, 'is it your place or mine?'

'Oh—it's Hanson Square,' she replied.

'It would be!'

CHAPTER TEN

THEY drove away from the restaurant and headed along the Chelsea Embankment. 'We have time, you and I', Bruce said. 'If you ever need me, or want me, then promise me to be in touch.'

'I promise, Bruce.'

'You have my address?'

'Well—no.'

'I have an apartment at Ranleigh Court in Knightsbridge, number twelve. You're more than welcome, Jorja.'

'You're kind to me and I appreciate it.'

'No,' he contradicted. 'I'm battening down the hatches on what I really want to do. It would be kinder in the long run if I took you anywhere but home to a marriage which is making you unhappy. Look, why not pack your belongings and get out? I'm not saying that you have to come home with me; I could book you into a hotel until you sort out in your mind what you really want to do. What do you say?'

'That I can't do it, Bruce. I can't add to what Renzo's going through. I have to stand by him.' She spoke almost with a touch of panic, as if he had suggested they stop and rob a bank.

'Do you expect any thanks for standing by?'

'Probably not, but it's going to be a difficult

time for him, especially as he's chosen not to try and locate Stelvio.'

'Who, presumably, is still with Angelica?'

'Yes.' She gazed through the wide windscreen, where she seemed to see Renzo's dark, determined face. She felt sure it was because of Angelica that he chose not to contact his brother, for who could tell what Stelvio might do? He might bring her to England with him!

'What are you thinking, Jorja?'

A traffic signal glowed red against the windscreen. 'That if I do leave Renzo, for whatever reason, then I shall go home to Duncton. You see, Bruce, I don't think love is for people like me. We take it too much to heart and want what is beyond the purely physical. Oh yes, everyone likes to make love but the real splendour is in feeling it.'

The traffic lights went from amber to green, and when the car arrived at Hanson Square and turned into the driveway of the house, Bruce looked at Jorja as if she had eluded him.

'I'll see you on Friday,' she said. 'Thank you for treating me to such a nice lunch.'

He gripped her hand, as if he would hold her there and not let her enter the tall Georgian house. 'If you go home to Duncton, then I'll follow you and prove how wrong you are to run away from me.'

'I must go in, Bruce.'

'Did you hear what I said, Jorja?'

'I heard, Bruce.'

'Would you refuse to see me if I came to the rectory?'

'Of course not.' She half-smiled. 'I'd give you lunch and return your hospitality.'

'You're an elusive girl, aren't you?'

'Which must be a novelty for a successful and attractive director of films,' she rejoined.

His green eyes glimmered down at her. 'So you think me attractive, eh?'

'You're a nice man, Bruce, but I'm a married woman and if I'm seen holding hands with you, right in front of my husband's house, I'm going to be in trouble. Do you want to make trouble for me?'

'Yes and no,' he said frankly. 'It would all be out in the open, wouldn't it?'

'Do let go of me, Bruce.'

'Must I really?'

'Yes.'

'You could invite me in.'

'I certainly won't.' She cast a swift look at the house, which had a serene and mellow look in the afternoon light; the emotions and sorrows it had witnessed were not apparent. The walls and windows were like features which had masked their pain.

'Renzo could have returned by now,' she said, dropping her voice into a lower key. 'If he has, then Monica will be with him.'

'It might make things easier for you if I came in,' Bruce suggested.

Jorja shook her head. 'You don't know the kind of mood Renzo has been in—I don't want him getting any wrong ideas about us.'

'Would they be so very wrong?'

'You know the answer to that.' She gave him a troubled look. 'I might not be the woman Renzo loves but I am his wife, and living in England doesn't mean that he reacts like an Englishman.'

'You're not afraid of him, are you?' Bruce glanced at the house, whose graciousness could be a kind of cage for Jorja. 'It was never my business to think of Renzo in relation to a woman, and I could certainly see that Angelica would be a match for Old Nick himself. But I'm damned if I'll have him pushing you around!'

'He doesn't push me around,' she protested.

'Not in a physical way, perhaps, but you're living on the edge of his moods, and you don't know how to please or console him, do you? To the devil with him, Jorja! You're not going into that house——'

At which juncture the front door opened above the steps to reveal Torrence. He came out in his stately way upon the top step. 'If you please, madam, you are wanted in the drawing-room.'

'Bruce,' her fingers scrabbled for their release, 'you must let go of me!'

'Let me come in——'

'No.' Her eyes flashed with appeal. 'I know you mean well, but you're going to get me into trouble—please, let me go.'

Reluctantly he let go of her hand and watched as she ran quickly up the steps and in through the door which Torrence held open. 'Thank you,' she said breathlessly to the butler. 'Signore Talmonte is back from the airport?'

'Yes, madam.' The butler quietly closed the door. 'He saw you from the drawing-room window and sent me to fetch you.'

Her heart was hammering. As she crossed the hall she heard the Porsche drive away and couldn't help feeling a stab of regret. Especially when she entered the room where Renzo stood tall and broodingly handsome by the windows, where the deep-gold of the curtains seemed to frame his dark-clad figure.

The moment she stepped into the drawing-room, his eyes ran over her, showing not a glimmer of welcome. 'Did you intend to stand all day in the square with Clayton?' he demanded. 'Hand in hand?'

'Bruce was good enough to give me lunch, and naturally he has offered his sympathy regarding your mother.' Jorja spoke composedly, but there was something in his manner which jarred on her. He had started to pace back and forth and when he gestured towards a chair, she obeyed him and sat down.

'Did you meet Monica?' she asked. 'Is she here?'

'Oh yes, she is here.'

His tone of voice was so sardonic that Jorja couldn't help looking at him in surprise. 'What is it, Renzo—what's wrong?' She felt instinctively that his manner had nothing to do with Bruce and the fact that she had spent two hours lunching with him. Something took precedence over that . . . something which she started to guess even as he began to tell her.

'Stelvio came with her,' he said, pausing in front of Jorja's chair and capturing her gaze, which widened incredulously upon his face. 'They are together right now in the guest suite, saying some of the things they couldn't discuss on the aircraft.'

'So Monica managed to contact him——?'

Renzo shook his head. 'It was Flavia. She assumed that I would want my brother located, so with her usual efficiency she proceeded to make enquiries. As it turned out he had left the yacht on which he had been cruising and had returned to Rome, and a business colleague was able to put Flavia in direct touch with him. She informed him that Monica was due to fly to London, gave him the time of the flight, and he was able to book himself a seat.'

Jorja sat there in silence, while all the unspoken questions raced through her mind. What about Angelica? Had Stelvio left the yacht because they had quarrelled? Had he even been on the yacht with her?

'Monica's with your brother in the guest suite?' she asked.

'They are together.' Renzo resumed his pacing. 'He's extremely upset over *madre*, but somehow it has bridged a very awkward gap. In a while they are going to the chapel of rest.'

'And what are you feeling, Renzo?' Jorja had to ask. 'You were so angry with him.'

Her husband spread his hands in a very Latin way. 'When I saw them together at the airport, what could I say? Monica was pleading with her eyes, and he was obviously stricken by the news about *madre*. And knowing our mother, she would want the two of us reconciled.'

'Oh, I'm glad about that.' Jorja rose to her feet and went to Renzo, her hand reaching out to his. It felt lean and muscular within her clasp, and it was the first time in days that she had touched him. 'I was hoping something like this would happen, for her sake.'

'I would prefer her to be alive.' He turned away from Jorja and went to stand alone by the window from which he had seen her with Bruce. '*Madre* was the one constant person in my life, always the same, always serene and wise. Other women? What are they? Creatures of the moment whom a man is a fool to trust.'

Jorja stared across the room at him, a slim figure in grey, uncertain as she stood beneath the charming, hand-painted scenes of Georgian court life which embellished the ceiling. A chill feeling struck through her, and suddenly she felt in the way. Like someone whose part in the drama was no longer integral to the plot.

'Renzo,' she had to ask, 'who walked out on whom?'

'Need you ask?' He went on gazing from the window into the square, where the sun had given way to the threat of rain.

'I see.' When Jorja stepped out of the drawing-room, a man and a woman were making their way downstairs. She was an elegant brunette wearing a black mink coat. He had something of Renzo in his appearance, but he seemed less distinct, certainly less impressive as he stood staring at Jorja.

Even as that look on his face slightly angered her, she realised that he hadn't expected his brother's wife to look like the woman who had almost ruined his marriage.

'I'm Jorja,' she said quietly. 'I'm glad you both had a safe journey to London.'

'I am glad to know you.' Monica stepped forward with a nervous eagerness and hugged Jorja against the silky dark fur of her coat. 'We are going to be friends, eh? We shall be a family again!'

Jorja was looking directly at Stelvio across Monica's shoulder and she saw a kind of resignation in his eyes; the look of a man who was here with his wife because he was no longer wanted elsewhere. He had been bewitched, led into the dance of love by Angelica . . . now the dance had ended but the spell of it still held him.

It was something Jorja had learned to live with, and she feared for the harmony which Monica hoped to enjoy with him.

Renzo's car and driver awaited them in the square, and after they had left for the chapel, Jorja went upstairs. She felt a little weary, as if her emotions had been stretched beyond bearing. She took off her shoes and jacket, stretched out on the couch in the sitting-room and closed her eyes. Her restless mind went back and forth over the events of the day, and each one had a significance which stretched beyond Friday, when both the Contessa's sons would now follow her casket to the quiet grave.

What, she wondered, had been Renzo's inmost thoughts when he had stood by the window and watched the day clouding over. He had not asked what she and Bruce had found to talk about, but he had probably watched them in some curiosity. He hadn't missed the way Bruce had held on to her hand.

She turned restlessly against the cushioned headrest of the couch. Did she want him to ask questions? Did she want him to show some sign of jealousy?

It was a forlorn hope. There was no jealousy without love or desire . . . no emotions of any sort between strangers, and in the past few days that was what they had become. Sometimes when she looked at him she saw again the cold stranger who had forced her to read Angelica's letters. The memory of it held Jorja like a stark dream, in which everything was darkly detailed. Even the roses seemed black in contrast to the torn-up pieces of paper on which words were still discernible.

'I need to be with you, Stelvio! When I'm in your arms and you are kissing every part of me, no one else matters! When you take me, I'm delirious . . .'

Jorja's lips twisted almost with cynicism. So much for the delirium of love! Where was Angelica right now? Was she with some other man, or were other plans going on in her lovely head?

Jorja listened to the sound of rain against the windows. Monica and Stelvio would be at the chapel right now, together in the dim, cool beauty of his mother's resting place. Her sad loss might bind him to his wife again, and in time he might forget the witchery and the self-serving lies of someone who looked like an angel and behaved like a devil.

Yes, there was a glimmer of hope for Monica and Stelvio, but Jorja saw no hope for her own marriage. It had never started out as a love affair; it had been for both of them a vendetta the impetus of which had died with the Contessa.

That was when Jorja had looked into Renzo's eyes and seen the pain and shock of a man affronted by his own behaviour, and from that moment he had shut her out. The rain was pelting the windows now, and the room had dimmed so that Jorja could barely make out its details. She was intensely startled when the telephone rang on the table beside the couch and for an instant she lay there, almost resenting its intrusion upon her thoughts.

When she lifted the receiver, she was even more startled to hear her husband's voice on the line. 'A friend of yours is calling,' he said. 'I'm switching him through to you.'

'Jorja?' As the caller spoke she heard Renzo replace the receiver of the downstair's phone. 'I just had to speak to you—I had to find out if you were all right. Are you?'

'Yes.' It was Bruce Clayton, and even as she automatically replied to him, she had an image of

Renzo, looking as he had sounded, neither angry nor amazed that Bruce should phone her. A cold, cold feeling swept through her, for his indifference was more punishing than anything else had ever been.

'Renzo saw us together, didn't he, Jorja?'

'Yes, he saw us from the window.'

'What did he have to say? Was he annoyed with you?'

'He didn't seem to care very much.' She shuddered anew and felt as if she were out in the rain and it was beating against her skin as it beat against the windows. 'He was back from the airport—Monica didn't come alone, Bruce. She came with Stelvio.'

'Stelvio? You mean he——'

'He had been in Rome for some days—alone.'

'Good lord! So the flaming affair with Angelica came to an end?'

'It would seem so.'

'Have you heard from her? Has she been in touch?'

'No.'

'You sound—what is it, Jorja, are you afraid of what she'll do?'

'I'm not afraid, Bruce, but I am prepared.'

'Damn that little hellcat! She hurts everyone she touches—leaves destruction in her path like some damned hurricane. You must get out of that house, Jorja! I'm coming to fetch you out before that sister of yours descends on you. You've done the unforgivable, haven't you? You've married one of her men, and they remain hers even after

she's turned them inside out. Pack a bag, Jorja. I'll
be with you in about twenty minutes——'

'No, Bruce . . .'

'See reason, my dear girl. Angelica's had a
game with Stelvio's heart, now she'll come after
Renzo again. You know it, and I know it. And
didn't you say that he still wants her?'

'I did say that, yes.'

'Then leave them to it. If Renzo still wants the
pain and dubious pleasure of Angelica, then walk
out on him, Jorja. Walk out with your head held
high. Let him see that you aren't beaten down.
Come away with me—you know I care about
you. You're the nicest, kindest, most sweet-face
girl I ever met and I want you—I want you, Jorja.'

'You're kind yourself, Bruce.'

'Then start packing that bag.'

'No.' Jorja surprised herself, she spoke the
word so firmly. 'I'm not running away.'

'You can't mean it. You can't stay and be torn in
two by a husband who doesn't love you, and a
sister who doesn't give a damn so long as her
whims and fancies are satisfied. You're not going
to like this, Jorja, but your sister's a film tramp.
She's appeared in the kind of movies they hire
out from way under the counter; the kind of
videos the police swoop down on.'

'I know,' Jorja said quietly. 'That's why I'm not
leaving Hanson Square, for I've the same feeling
you have, Bruce. I believe she's back in London
—she's out there somewhere, among the glaring
lights, and she's looking this way.'

'God, Jorja, you're making my blood run cold,'

Bruce exclaimed. 'What are you going to do?'

'I'll kill her,' Jorja said deliberately, 'if she tries to lay one hand on Renzo.'

There was a protracted silence at the other end of the telephone line, then Bruce spoke and the energy had drained out of his voice. 'You love him that much, Jorja?'

'It seems that I do, Bruce.' Energy was flowing in her own voice; flowing through her, warming her back to life again. 'A little while ago I was lying here on the couch and I had the surest feeling that I'm going to have a baby. It wasn't anything tangible, no sudden faintness, or sudden craving for spicy pickles, just a tiny finger touching my heart and warning me not to give up what became mine on the day I promised to love, cherish and keep for always the man I married.'

'But he forced you into marriage with him,' Bruce protested.

'There's no doubt of that,' she agreed. 'But he never forced me into his arms, I went willingly.'

A quiet groan broke from Bruce Clayton. 'What's the scenario if he tells you to your face that he doesn't want you?'

'He'll want his child.'

'And you'll settle for that?'

'If I must.'

'You're a sweet-faced fool, Jorja.'

'I dare say I am, but I know something wise, that very often in a family a baby replaces a beloved person who has died, and I shall be as ruthless as Angelica in getting what I want. Believe me, Bruce.'

'It seems I have to believe you, dearest girl, who will never be my dear.'

'Thank you for phoning me, dear Bruce.'

'Was my call the catalyst which made up your mind?'

'Yes.' And she was smiling in the darkness as she cradled the receiver and rose to her feet. After switching on the light she found her shoes and stepped into them. She smoothed her hair but didn't look at herself in the mirror; right now she didn't want to face those aspects which made her look like Angelica. She was Jorja, and as Jorja she was going to confront Renzo.

Upon arriving downstairs, where the lights were ablaze in the hall, she glanced into the drawing-room but found it unoccupied. She went across to the music-room and opened the door with its rococo carvings of tiny fiddles, trumpets and harps. The handsome grand piano stood as silent as the recording equipment, and on the music stand there was a half-filled page of those strange symbols which turned out to be the most sweeping and romantic of harmonies.

Had he left the house? Had he gone out in the rain, to walk down to the Embankment to stand alone with his thoughts?

'Are you looking for your husband, madam?'

She turned to face Torrence, and instantly she had composed her features. 'Has he gone out?' she asked.

'No, madam, he asked for coffee to be served to him in the garden room.

'I'll join him.'

As she made her way to the garden room, Jorja felt that Torrence was concerned for her. He would have noticed the constraint between Renzo and herself, and the maids would have mentioned that they weren't sharing a bed. Jorja suddenly knew how much she wanted her husband's arms around her; she wanted the close, hard feel of him, his deep-grey eyes flickering with fire as he touched her, kissed her, made her belong to him from her tingling toes to the luxurious movements of her head, cradled by his arm.

He sat in the high-backed cane chair, the lamp-light softened by the amber shade. He gazed out upon the dark, wet garden and despite his look of being alone with thoughts he didn't wish to share, Jorja felt only a momentary pang of hesitation.

'May I sit with you, Renzo?' And without waiting for his reply, she approached him and sat down on the foot of the chaise-longue. 'I can smell the rain on the grass. It's such a wonderful smell, isn't it?'

'Innocent,' he said, 'like the beginning of the world.'

'Sometimes you say things that are like your music.'

'The better part of me speaking.'

'We're all shaded in by the lights and darks of our personalities,' she said, clasping her arms about her knees because they trembled just a fraction. 'There aren't many people whom the Devil's Advocate would be able to pronounce as saintly.'

'Not many,' he agreed, 'but there are those who don't deserve to be hurt. Those who give of themselves without asking the one who takes if he deserves such generosity——'

Suddenly, to Jorja's deep distress, a sob broke from Renzo, and instantly she was on her feet and she was holding him, pressing his head to her breast, stroking his black hair and murmuring his name.

'Renzo, darling, what can I do to help you? I know how much you are grieving for your mother.'

He shook his head against her. 'It isn't *madre*, not entirely.'

'Then tell me, dear heart.'

'How can you call me that?' he burst out. 'How can you bear to be near me? Why aren't you with Bruce? He phoned you—he wanted you—don't you think I could tell?'

'Yes, he phoned because he thought I was leaving you.'

'So that was what you talked about over your lunch with him?' But even as he spoke, Renzo clasped his arms about her waist and his entire body strained for her closeness and her touch.

'We talked about a lot of things, Renzo, and I told him that if I left you I would go home to Duncton because love is something I don't seem able to cope with. But that was at lunchtime. I didn't know then what I know now, that love has a further side to it, one that doesn't give up what it feels is worth fighting for.'

She paused and slowly ran her fingers down

his face, feeling the hard fine bone of him and the heat of his lips. 'Angelica,' she said deliberately, 'can go to hell. I can give you more, and beyond that more than she ever can. I'll fight her tooth and nail if she comes anywhere near the man who belongs to me.'

Her breast heaved as she spoke, and then she felt lips hard and urgent against her body. She felt him standing, taking hold of her, lifting her and laying her down on the chaise-longue. His lips were bruising her, but it was wonderful. His hands were everywhere, and it was doubly wonderful.

'Jorja, *dolce mia,*' he explored her as if he had just found her, as if she were his brand new bride and he had never known her. In a mixture of Italian and English he said things that brought the heat rushing to her face.

'After the destructiveness of Angelica how could I believe that her sister could be so beneficent? Like some damned, ungrateful brute I started to look for faults in you. How could I do it? What got into me? Here, here in this garden room I lashed out at you and your sweet young face went so white. *Madre* was angry with me and it may have been what I did, what I said to you that brought on her heart attack!'

'No.' Jorja pressed a kiss against his mouth. 'When I phoned the doctor he seemed as if he'd been expecting such a call. I believe, Renzo dear, that your mother was dying and she wanted to be with you. The three of us were together, weren't we? She knew and spoke of being contented, didn't she? She couldn't take any more suffering, for there is a point beyond bearing and when we reach it, Renzo, we die.'

After long, long moments he spoke. 'If your love for me has died, then tell me. I don't want pretence, or sacrifice, or anything that isn't total need and desire. I want every tiny atom of what you are. Every breath in your body. Every smile that you smile. Every joy and pain.'

He drew her to his heart, savage and tender . . . as love is.

'We get the measure of the love we give,' she said softly. 'Love me with all your heart, and in return I shall love with all my heart all and every atom of you.'

He searched her eyes in the lamplight and they were clear and bright as the night had become, there beyond the windows of the garden room. The rain had died away and the clouds had unveiled a slip of a moon. It peered in through the windows, almost like a smile that watched as a lover kissed his love.